THE SKY-LINERS

This Large Print Book carries the
Seal of Approval of N.A.V.H.

LOUIS L'AMOUR

THE SKY-LINERS

THORNDIKE PRESS • THORNDIKE, MAINE

Library of Congress Cataloging in Publication Data:

L'Amour, Louis, 1908-
   The sky-liners / Louis L'Amour.
      p. cm.
   ISBN 1-56054-650-6 (alk. paper : lg. print)
   1. Large type books. I. Title.
[PS3523.A446S57   1993]   92-42376
813'.52—dc20   CIP

Thorndike Large Print® Special Series edition published
in 1993 by arrangement with Bantam Books, Inc.

Cover design by Abby Trudeau.
Cover illustration by Deborah Pompano.

The tree indicium is a trademark of Thorndike Press.

This book is printed on acid-free, high opacity paper. ∞

THE SKY-LINERS

Chapter 1

Everyone in our part of the country knew of Black Fetchen, so folks just naturally stood aside when he rode into town with his kinfolk.

The Fetchen land lay up on Sinking Creek, and it wasn't often a Sackett got over that way, so we had no truck with one another. We heard talk of him and his doings — how he'd killed a stranger over on Caney's Fork, and about a fair string of shootings and cuttings running back six or seven years.

He wasn't the only Fetchen who'd worked up to trouble in that country, or down in the flat land, for that matter. It was a story told and retold how Black Fetchen rode down to Tazewell and taken some kin of his away from the law.

James Black Fetchen his name was, but all knew him as Black, because the name suited.

He was a dark, handsome man with a bold, hard-shouldered way about him, as quick with his fists as with a gun. Those who rode with him, like Tory Fetchen and Colby Rafin, were the same sort.

Me and Galloway had business over in Tazewell or we'd never have been around those parts, not that we feared Black Fetchen, or any man, but we were newly home from the western lands and when we went to Tazewell we went to pay off the last of Pa's debts. Pa had bad luck several years running and owed honor debts we were bound to pay, so Galloway and me rode back from the buffalo plains to settle up.

We had taken off to the western lands two years before, me twenty-two then and him twenty-one. We worked the Santa Fe Trail with a freight outfit, and laid track for a railroad mountain spur, and finally went over the trail from Texas with a herd of steers. It wasn't until we went buffalo hunting that we made our stake.

About that time we heard some kinfolk of ours, name of William Tell Sackett, was herding up trouble down in the Mogollon, so we saddled up and lit out, because when a Sackett has trouble his kin is just bound to share it with him. So we rode down to help him clean things up.

This debt in Tazewell now was the last, and

our last cent as well. After two years we were right back where we started, except that we had our rifles and hand guns, and a blanket or two. We'd sold our horses when we came back to Tennessee from the hunting grounds.

We walked across the mountain, and when we got to town we headed for the town pump. Once we'd had a drink we started back across the street to settle our debt at the store that had given Pa credit when times were bad.

We were fairly out in the middle of the street when hoofs began to pound and a passel of folks a-horseback came charging up, all armed and loaded for feudin' or bear-fightin'.

Folks went high-tailing it for shelter when they saw those riders coming, but we were right out in the middle of the street and of no mind to run. They came a-tearing down upon us and one of them taken a cut at me with a quirt, yelling, "Get outen the street!"

Well, I just naturally reached up and grabbed a hold on that quirt, and most things I lay a hand to will move. He had a loop around his wrist and couldn't let go if he was a mind to, so I just jerked and he left that saddle a-flying and landed in the dust. The rest of them, they reined around, of a mind to see some fun.

That one who sat in the dust roosted there a

9

speck, trying to figure what happened to him, and then he came off the ground with a whoop and laid at me with a fist.

Now, we Sacketts had always been handy at knuckle-and-skull fighting, but Galloway and me had put in a spell with Irish track-layers and freighting teamsters who did most of their fighting like that. When this stranger looped a swing at my face, I just naturally stepped inside and clobbered him with a short one.

I fetched him coming in on me, and his head snapped back as if you'd laid the butt end of an axe against it. He went into the dust and about that time I heard Galloway saying, mild-like, "Go ahead, if you're a mind to. I'm takin' bets I can empty four, five saddles before you get me."

Me, I'd held my own rifle in my left hand this while, so I just flipped her up, my hand grasped the action, and I was ready. The two of us stood there facing the nine of them and it looked like blood on the ground.

Only nobody moved.

The big, handsome man who had been riding point for the outfit looked us over and said, "I'm Black Fetchen."

Galloway, he spoke over to me. "Black Fetchen, he says. Flagan, are you scared?"

"Don't seem to be, now that I think on it. But I've been scared a time or two. Recall that

Comanche out there on the short grass? There for a minute or two I figured he had me."

"But you fetched him, Flagan. Now, what all do you figure we should do with this lot?"

"Well, he made his confession. He owned up fair and honest who he was. He never tried to lie out of it. You got to give credit to a man who'll confess like that."

"Maybe" – Galloway was almighty serious – "but I think you're mistaken in this man. He owned up to the fact that he was Black Fetchen, but there wasn't the shame in him there should have been. I figure a man who can up and say 'I'm Black Fetchen' should feel shame. Might at least hang his head and scuff his toe a mite."

Black Fetchen had been growing madder by the minute. "I've had enough of this! By the –!"

"Hold off, Black." That was Colby Rafin talking. "I seen these two before, over nigh the Gap. These are Sacketts. I heard tell they'd come home from the buffalo range."

Now, we Sacketts have been feuding up and down the country with one outfit or another for nigh on to a hundred years, and nobody could say we hadn't marked up our share of scalps, but nobody could say that we hunted trouble.

When Rafin said that, we could just sort of see Black Fetchen settling down into his saddle.

11

We weren't just a pair of green mountain boys putting on a show. He was a brave man, but only a fool will chance a shot from a Winchester at forty feet. Knowing who we were, he now knew we would shoot, so he sat quiet and started to smile. "Sorry, boys, but a joke is a joke. We've come to town on business and want no trouble. Shall I say we apologize?"

That was like a rattlesnake stopping his rattling while keeping his head drawn back to strike.

"You can say that," I agreed, "and we'll accept it just like you mean it; but just so's there's no misunderstanding, why don't you boys just shuck your artillery? Just let them fall gentle into the street."

"I'll be damned if I will!" Tory Fetchen yelled.

"You'll be dead if you don't," Galloway told him. "As to being damned, you'll have to take that up with your Lord and Maker. You going to shuck those guns, or do I start shooting?"

"Do what he says, boys," Black said. "This is only one day. There'll be another."

They did as ordered, but Galloway is never one to let things be. He's got a hankering for the fringe around the edges.

"Now, Gentlemen and Fellow-Sinners, you have come this day within the shadow of the valley. It is well for each and everyone of us to recall how weak is the flesh, how close we stand to Judgment, so you will all join me in singing 'Rock of Ages.' "

He gestured to Black Fetchen. "You will lead the singing, and I hope you are in fine voice."

"You're crazy!"

"Maybe," Galloway agreed, "but I want to hear you loud and clear. You got until I count three to start, and you better make sure they all join in."

"Like hell!" Tory was seventeen, and he was itching to prove himself as tough as he thought he was . . . or as tough as he wanted others to think he was.

Galloway fired, and that bullet whipped Tory's hat from his head and notched his ear. "Sing, damn you!" Galloway said; and brother, they sang.

I'll say this for them, they had good strong voices and they knew the words. Up in the mountains the folks are strong on goin' to meetin', and these boys all knew the words. We heard it clear: *Rock of ages, cleft for me, Let me hide, myself in thee.*

"Now you all turn around," Galloway advised, "and ride slow out of town. I want all these good people to know you ain't bad boys — just sort of rambunctious when there's nobody

13

about to discipline you a mite."

"Your guns," I said, "will be in the bank when it opens tomorrow!"

So James Black Fetchen rode out of town with all that rowdy gang of his, and we stood with our rifles and watched them go.

"Looks like we made us some enemies, Flagan," Galloway said.

"Sufficient to the day is the evil thereof," I commented, liking the mood, "but don't you mind. We've had enemies before this."

We collected the guns and deposited them in the bank, which was closing, and then we walked across the street and settled Pa's account.

Everybody was chuckling over what happened, but also they warned us of what we could expect. We didn't have cause to expect much, for the fact was we were going back to the buffalo prairies. Back home there was nothing but an empty cabin, no meat in the pot, no flour in the bin.

We had done well our first time west, and now we would go back and start over. Besides, there were a lot of Sackett kinfolk out there now.

We started off.

Only we didn't get far. We had just reached the far end of town when we sighted a camp at the edge of the woods, and an oldish man walked out to meet us. We'd talked with enough Irish lads whilst working on the railroad to recognize the brogue. "May I be havin' a word wi' you, boys?"

So we stopped, with Galloway glancing back up the street in case those Fetchen boys came back with guns.

"I'm Laban Costello," he said, "and I'm a horse-trader."

More than likely everybody in the mountains knew of the Irish horse-traders. There were eight families of them, good Irish people, known and respected throughout the South. They were drifting folk, called gypsies by some, and they moved across the land swapping horses and mules, and a canny lot they were. It was in my mind this would be one of them.

"I am in trouble," he said, "and my people are far away in Atlanta and New Orleans."

"We are bound for the buffalo lands, but we would leave no man without help. What can we do?"

"Come inside," he said, and we followed him back into the tent.

This was like no tent I had ever seen, with rugs on the ground and a curtained wall across one side to screen off a sleeping space. This was the tent of a man who moved often, but lived well wherever he stopped. Out behind it we had noticed a caravan wagon, painted and bright.

Making coffee at the fire was a girl, a pretty sixteen by the look of her. Well, maybe she was pretty. She had too many freckles, and a pert, sassy way about her that I didn't cotton to.

"This is my son's daughter," he said. "This is Judith."

"Howdy, ma'am," Galloway said.

Me, I merely looked at her and she wrinkled her nose at me. I turned away sharp, ired by any fool slip of a girl so impolite as to do such as that to a stranger.

"First, let me say that I saw what happened out there in the street, and you are the first who have faced up to Fetchen in a long while. He is a bad man, a dangerous man."

"We ain't likely to see him again," I said, "for we are bound out across the plains."

Personally, I wanted him to get to the point. It was my notion those Fetchens would borrow guns and come back, loaded for bear and Sacketts. This town was no place to start a shooting fight, and I saw no cause to fight when nothing was at stake.

"Have you ever been to Colorado?"

"Nigh to it. We have been in New Mexico."

"My son lives in Colorado. Judith is his daughter."

Time was a-wasting and we had a far piece to go. Besides, I was getting an uneasy feeling about where all this was leading.

"It came to me," Costello said, "that as you are going west, and you Sacketts have the name of honorable men, I might prevail upon you to escort my son's daughter to her father's home."

"No," I said.

"Now, don't be hasty. I agree that traveling with a young girl might seem difficult, but Judith has been west before, and she has never known any other life but the camp and the road."

"She's been west?"

"Her father is a mustanger, and she traveled with him."

"Hasn't she some folks who could take her west?" I asked. Last thing I wanted was to have a girl-child along, making trouble, always in the way, and wanting special treatment.

"At any other time there would be plenty, but now there is no time to waste. You see Black Fetchen had put his mind to her."

"Her?" I was kind of contemptuous. "Why, she ain't out of pigtails yet!"

She stuck out her tongue at me, but I paid her no mind. What worried me was that Galloway wasn't speaking up. He was just listening, and every once in a while he'd look at that snip of a girl.

17

"She will be sixteen next month, and many a girl is wed before the time. Black Fetchen has seen her and has told me he means to have her . . . in fact, he had come tonight to take her, but you stopped him before he reached us."

"Sorry," I told him, "but we've got to travel fast, and we may have a shooting fight with those Fetchens before we get out of Tennessee. They don't shape up to be a forgiving lot."

"You have horses?"

"Well, no. We sold them back in Missouri to pay up what Pa owed hereabouts. We figured to join up with a freight outfit we once worked with, and get west to New Mexico. There's Sacketts out there where we could get some horses until time we could pay for them."

"Suppose I provide the horses? Or rather, suppose Judith does? She owns six head of mighty fine horses, and where she goes, they go."

"No," I said.

"You have seen Fetchen. Would you leave a young girl to him?"

He had me there. I wouldn't leave a yeller hound dog to that man. He was big, and fierce-looking for all he was so handsome, but he looked to me like a horse- and wife-beater, and I'd met up with a few.

"The townsfolk wouldn't stand for that," I said.

"They are afraid of him. As for that, he says he wishes to marry Judith. As far as the town goes, we are movers. We don't belong to the town."

It wasn't going to be easy for us, even without a girl to care for. We would have to hunt for what we ate, sleep out in the open, dodge Indians, and make our way through some of the worst possible country. If we tied on with a freight outfit we would be with rough men, in a rough life. Traveling like that, a girl would invite trouble, and it appeared we would have a-plenty without that.

"Sorry," I said.

"There is one other thing," Costello said. "I am prepared to give each of you a fine saddle horse and a hundred dollars each to defray expenses on the way west."

"We'll do it," Galloway said.

"Now, see here," I started to protest, but they were no longer listening. I have to admit that he'd knocked my arguments into a cocked hat by putting up horses and money. With horses, we could ride right on through, not having to tie up with anybody, and the money would pay for what we needed. Rustling grub for ourselves wouldn't amount to much. But I still didn't like it. I didn't figure to play nursemaid to any girl.

"The horses are saddled and ready. Judith will ride one of her own, and her gear will be on another. And there will be four pack horses if you want to use them as such."

"Look," I said. "That girl will be trouble enough, but you said those horses of hers were breeding stock. Aside from the geldings you'll be giving us, we'll have a stallion and five mares, and that's trouble in anybody's country."

"The stallion is a pet. Judith has almost hand-fed it since it was a colt."

"Ma'am," I turned on her. "That stallion will get itself killed out yonder. Stallions, wild stock, will come for miles to fight him, and some of them are holy terrors."

"You don't have to worry about Ram," she replied. "He can take care of himself."

"This here girl," I argued, "she couldn't stand up to it. West of the river there ain't a hotel this side of the Rockies fit for a lady, and we figure to sleep under the stars. There'll be dust storms and rainstorms, hail the like of which you never saw; and talk about thunder and lightning . . ."

Costello was smiling at me. "Mr. Sackett, you seem to forget to whom you are talking. We are of the Irish horse-traders. I doubt if Judith has slept under a roof a dozen times in her life, other than the roof of a caravan. She has lived in the saddle since she could walk, and will ride as well as either of you."

Well, that finished me off. Ride as well as me? Or Galloway? That was crazy.

"Look," I said to Galloway, "we can't take no girl."

"Where else are we going to get horses and an outfit?" he interrupted.

He was following Costello out the back way, and there were eight horses, saddled, packed and ready, standing under the poplars. And eight finer animals you never did see. Nobody ever lived who was a finer judge of horseflesh than those Irish traders, and these were their own stock, not for trading purposes.

Right off I guessed them to be Irish hunters with a mite of some other blood. Not one of them was under sixteen hands, and all were splendidly built. The sight of those horses started me weakening almighty fast. I'd never seen such horses, and had never owned anything close to the one he'd picked for me.

"Irish hunters," he said, "with a judicious mixture of mustang blood. We did the mustanging ourselves, or rather, Judith and her father and his brother did. They kept the best of the mustangs for breeding, because we wanted horses with stamina as well as speed, and horses that could live off the country.

21

Believe me, these horses are just what we wanted."

"I'd like to," I said, "but —"

"Fetchen wants these horses," Costello added, "and as they belong to Judith and her father, they would go with her."

"That makes sense," I said. "Now I can see why Fetchen wanted her."

She was standing close by and she hauled off and kicked me on the shin. I yelped, and they all turned to look to me. "Nothing," I said. "It wasn't anything."

"Then you had better ride out of here," Costello said; "but make no mistake. Black Fetchen will come after you. Today was the day Fetchen was coming after Judith."

When I threw a leg over that black horse and settled down into the leather I almost forgave that Judith. This was more horse than I'd ever sat atop of. It made a man proud. No wonder Fetchen wanted that fool girl, if he could get these horses along with her.

We taken out.

Galloway led the way, keeping off the road and following a cow path along the stream.

When we were a mile or so out of town, Galloway edged over close to me. "Flagan, there's one thing you don't know. We got to watch that girl. Her grandpa whispered it to me. She thinks highly of Black Fetchen. She figures he's romantic — dashing and all that. We've got to watch her, or she'll slip off and go back."

Serve her right, I thought.

Chapter 2

Now, there's no accounting for the notions of womenfolks, particularly when they are sixteen. She came of good people. We Sacketts had dealt with several generations of Irish horse-traders, and found them sharp dealers, but so were we all when it came to swapping horseflesh. There were several thousand of them, stemming from the eight original families, and it was a rare thing when one married outside the clans.

I thought about Black Fetchen. To give the devil his due, I had to admit he was a bold and handsome man, and a fine horseman. He was hell on wheels in any kind of a fight, and his kinfolk were known for their rowdy, bullying ways. Judith had seen Fetchen ride into town, all dressed up and flashy, with a lot of push and swagger to him. She knew nothing of the killings behind him.

We rode a goodly distance, holding to mountain trails. Judith rode along meek as a lamb, and when we stopped I figured she was plumb wore out. She ate like a hungry youngster, but she was polite as all get out, and that should have warned me. After I banked the fire I followed Galloway in going to sleep. Judith curled up in a blanket close by.

The thing is, when a man hunts out on the buffalo grass he gets scary. If he sleeps too sound he can lose his hair, so a body gets fidgety in his sleep, waking up every little while, and ready to come sharp awake if anything goes wrong.

Of a sudden, I woke up. A thin tendril of smoke lifted from the banked fire, and I saw that Judith was gone. I came off the ground, stamped into my boots, and grabbed my pistol belt.

It took me a minute to throw on a saddle and cinch up, then I lit out of there as if the devil was after me. The tracks were plain to see. There was no need to even tell Galloway, because when he awakened he could read the sign as easy as some folks would read a book.

She had led her horse a good hundred yards away from camp, and then she had mounted up, held her pace down for a little bit further, and then started to canter.

At the crossing of the stream the tracks

turned toward the highroad, and I went after her. For half a mile I let that black horse run, and he had it in him to go. Then I eased down and took my rope off the saddle and shook out a loop.

She heard me coming and slapped her heels to her horse, and for about two miles we had us the prettiest horse race you ever did see.

The black was too fast for her, and as we closed in I shook out a loop and dabbed it over her shoulders. The black was no roping horse, but when I pulled him in that girl left her horse a-flyin' and busted a pretty little dent in the ground when she hit stern first.

She came off the ground fighting mad, but I'd handled too many fractious steers to be bothered by that, so before she knew what was happening I had her hog-tied and helpless.

For a female youngster, she had quite a surprising flow of language, shocking to a man of my sensibilities, and no doubt to her under other circumstances. She'd been around horse-trading men since she was a baby, and she knew all the words and the right emphasis.

Me, I just sat there a-waiting while she fussed at me. I taken off my hat, pushed back my hair, settled my hat on my head again, all the time seeming to pay her no mind. Then I swung down from the saddle and picked her up and slung her across her horse, head and heels hanging. And then we trotted back to camp.

Galloway was saddled up and ready to ride. "What all you got there, boy?" he called to me.

"Varmint. I ketched it down the road a piece. Better stand shy of it because I figure it'll bite, and might have a touch of hydrophoby, judgin' by sound."

Wary of heels and teeth, I unslung her from the saddle. "Ma'am, I'm of no mind to treat anybody thisaway, but you brought it on yourself. Now, if you'll set easy in the saddle I'll unloose you."

Well, she spoke her piece for a few minutes and then she started to cry, and that done it. I unloosed her, helped her into the saddle, and we started off again, with her riding peaceable enough.

"You just wait," she said. "Black Fetchen will come. He will come riding to rescue me."

"You or the horses," I said. "I hear he's a man sets store by good horseflesh."

"He will come."

"You'd best hope he doesn't, ma'am," Galloway suggested. "We promised to deliver you to your pa in Colorado, and that's what we aim to do."

"If he really loves you," I said, "he'd think nothing of riding to Colorado. Was I in love

27

with a girl, that would seem a short way to go."

"*You!*" she said scornfully. "Who would ever love *you?*"

Could be she was totally right, but I didn't like to think it. Nobody ever did love me that I could remember of, except Ma. Galloway, he was a rare hand with the girls, but not me. I never knew how to sit up and carry on with them, and likely they thought me kind of stupid. Hard to find two brothers more alike and more different than Galloway and me.

Both of us were tall and raw-boned, only he was a right handsome man with a lot of laughter in him, and easy-talking except in times of trouble. Me, I was quieter, and I never smiled much. I was taller than Galloway by an inch, and there was an arrow scar on my cheekbone, picked up on the Staked Plains from a Comanche brave.

We grew up on a sidehill farm in the mountains, fourteen miles from a crossroads store and twenty miles from a town — or what passed as such. We never had much, but there was always meat on the table. Galloway and me, we shot most of our eatin' from the time I was six and him five, and many a time we wouldn't have eaten at all if we couldn't shoot.

Ma, she was a flatland schoolma'am until she up and married Pa and came to live in the mountains, and when we were growing up she tried to teach us how to talk proper. We both came to writing and figuring easy enough, but we talked like the boys around us. Although when it came right down to it, both of us could talk a mite of language, Galloway more than me.

Mostly Ma was teaching us history. In the South in those days everybody read Sir Walter Scott, and we grew up on *Ivanhoe* and the like. She had a sight of other books, maybe twenty all told, and one time or another we read most of them. After Ma died, me and Galloway batched it alone until we went west.

Galloway and me were Injun enough to leave mighty little trail behind us. We held to high country when possible, and we fought shy of traveled roads. Nor did we head for Independence, which was what might have been expected.

We cut across country, leaving the Kentucky border behind, and along Scaggs' Creek to Barren River, but just before the Barren joined the Green we cut back, west by a mite south, for Smithland, where the Cumberland joined the Ohio. It did me good to ride along Scaggs' Creek, because the Scaggs it was named for had been a Long Hunter in the same outfit with one of the first of my family to come over the mountains.

We bought our meals from farms along the way, or fixed our own. We crossed the Mississippi a few miles south of St. Louis.

No horses could have been better than those we had. They were fast walkers, good travelers, and always ready for a burst of speed when called upon.

Judith was quiet. Her eyes got bigger and rounder, it seemed to me, and she watched our back trail. She was quick to do what she ought and never complained, which should have been a warning. When she did talk it was to Galloway. To me she never said aye, yes, or no.

"What is it like out there?" she asked him.

"Colorado? It's a pure and lovely land beyond the buffalo grass where the mountains r'ar up to the sky. Snow on 'em the year 'round, and the mountains yonder make our Tennessee hills look like dirt thrown up by a gopher.

"It's a far, wide land with the long grass rippling in the wind like a sea with the sun upon it. A body can ride for weeks and see nothing but prairie and sky . . . unless, it's wild horses or buffalo."

"Are the women pretty?"

"Women? Ma'am, out in that country a body won't see a woman in months, 'less it's some old

a bit, I made him out, a crawling man,
ny yards off. Carefully, I looked all
at the night, but I saw nothing.
ped back to camp. "Galloway," I whis-
there's a man out yonder, sounds to be
d. I'm going to bring him in."

go ahead. I'll stand by."

was a trick, somebody would wish it
I walked out there, spotted the man
nd spoke to him quiet-like, so's my voice
't carry.

at's the trouble, *amigo*?"

crawling stopped, and for a moment
was silence. Then the voice came, low,
sational. "I've caught a bad one. Figured
psed a fire."

bein' sought after?"
ely."

I went up to him then and picked him
packed him into camp. He was a man of
r so, with a long narrow face and a black
che streaked with gray. He had caught a
ne through the body and he looked
y peaked. The slug had gone on through,
was holed on both sides. Whilst I set to
ng him up, Galloway, he moved out to
n eye on the prairie.

th, she woke up and set to making some
oth, and by the time I'd patched him up

squaw or an oldish white woman . . . or maybe a dancing girl in some saloon. Mostly a man just thinks about women, and they all get to look mighty fine after a while. A body forgets how mean and contrary they can be, and he just thinks of them as if they were angels or something."

We saw no sign of Black Fetchen nor any of his lot, yet I'd a notion they were closing in behind us. He didn't look like a man to be beaten, and we had stood him up in his own street, making him lose face where folks would tell of it, and we had taken his girl and the horses he wanted.

There was more to it than that, but we did not know it until later.

From time to time Judith talked some to Galloway, and we heard about her pa and his place in Colorado. Seems he'd left the horse-trading for mustanging, and then drifted west and found himself a ranch in the wildest kind of country. He started breeding horses, but kept on with the mustanging. Judith he'd sent back to be with his family and get some education. Only now he wanted her out there with him.

Now and again some of the family went west and often they drove horses back from his ranch to trade through the South. But now he wanted his daughter, and the stock she would bring with her.

Back of it all there was a thread of something that worried me. Sizing it up, I couldn't find anything that didn't sound just right, but there it was. Call it a hunch if you like, but I had a feeling there was something wrong in Colorado. Galloway maybe felt the same, but he didn't speak of it any more than me.

We camped out on the prairie. It was Indian country, only most of the Indians were quiet about that time. Farmers were moving out on the land, but there were still too many loose riders, outlaws from down in the Nation, and others no better than they should be. This was a stretch of country I never did cotton to, this area between the Mississippi and the real West. It was in these parts that the thieves and outlaws got together.

Not that Galloway or me was worried. We figured to handle most kinds of trouble. Only thing was, we had us a girl to care for . . . one who would grab hold of a horse any time she saw a chance and head for home . . . and Black Fetchen.

One night we camped on the Kansas prairie with a moon rising over the far edge of the world and stars a-plenty. We could hear the sound of the wind in the grass and stirring leaves of the cottonwoods under which we had

camped. It was a corner ᵢ extent, at a place where a a big boulder. There wa that boulder where we sh there was a fallen tree, anᴅ limbs.

We built up a small fire, our beef and beans we sat ᵃ of the old songs, the mour them reaching back to the came across the water fror

Judith was singing, too, aₙ she had, better than either sing, but weren't much acᴄ

The horses moved in close the voices. It was a mighty Judith turned in, Galloway the first watch. Taking up ₙ around outside the trees of

Second time around I pulle the west side. Something wa der in the dark, and I squatt closer to the ground, to hear grass.

Something was coming slᴏ hurt, by the sound of it. The dragging movement, and a tim faint groan. But I made no trusting no such sound.

she was about ready with it. I figured he'd lost blood, so I mixed up some salt water and had him drink that. We had been doing that for lost blood for years back, and it seemed to help.

He was game, I'll say that for him. Whilst Judith fed soup into him, I had a look at his foot.

"Wagon tongue fell on it," he said. "Rider jumped his horse into camp and knocked the wagon tongue over and she hit me on the instep."

His foot was badly swollen, and I had to cut the boot off. He stared at me between swallows of soup. "Look at that now!" he worried. "Best pair of boots I ever did have! Bought 'em a month back in Fort Worth."

"You a Texan?"

"Not reg'lar. I'm an Arkansawyer. I been cookin' for a cow outfit trailin' stock up from the Neuces country. Last evenin' a man stopped by our wagon for a bite of grub. He was a lean, dark, thin sort of man with narrow eyes. He was rough-dressed, but he didn't look western." He glanced up, suddenly wary. "Fact is, he talked somewhat like you boys."

"Don't be troubled. There's no kin of ours about here."

"He wore a sort of red sash and carried a rifle like he was born to it —"

"Colby Rafin!" Judith said.

"You called it, I didn't," I said.

"Anyway, he et and then rode off. About the time we'd been an hour abed, they come a-hellin' out of the night. Must've been a dozen of them or twenty. They come chargin' through camp, a-shootin' and a-yellin' and they drove off our herd, drove them to hell off down the country."

"You'd better catch some rest. You look done in."

He looked straight at me. "I ain't a-gonna make it, *amigo*, an' you know it."

Judith, she looked at me, all white and funny, but I said to him, "You got anybody you want us to tell?"

"I got no kin. Bald-Knobbers killed them all, a long time back. Down Texas way my boss was Evan Hawkes, a fine man. He lost a sight out there this night — his herd, his outfit, and his boy."

"Boy?"

"Youngster . . . mebbe thirteen. He had been beggin' the boss to let him ride north with us instead of on the cars. We were to meet Hawkes in Dodge."

"Are you sure about the boy?"

"Seen him fall. A man shot right into him, rode over him. If any of our outfit got away it was one of the boys on night herd."

He sat quiet for a while, and I stole a glance at Judith. She was looking almighty serious, and she had to realize that bunch of raiders that stole the herd and killed the boy had been the Fetchen outfit. Colby Rafin was never far from Black.

"They know they got you?"

"Figured it. They knew I was knocked down by the wagon tongue, and then one of them shot into me as he jumped his horse over."

As carefully as I could, I was easing the biggest sticks away from the fire so it would burn down fast. One thing was sure. That Fetchen outfit had followed us west. But this was no place or time to have a run-in with them.

The man opened his eyes after a bit and looked at Judith. "Ma'am? In my shirt pocket I got a gold locket. Ain't much, mebbe, but my ma wore it her life long, and her ma before her. I'd take it kindly, if you'd have it as a present."

"Yes . . . thank you."

"You got tender hands, ma'am, mighty gentle hands. Been a long time since a woman touched me . . . gentlelike. It's a fine thing to remember, ma'am."

I'd moved off to the edge of the darkness, listening for trouble riding our way, but I could faintly hear him still talking. "That tall man here," he said, "he carries the look of an eagle. He'll make tracks in the land, ma'am. You better latch onto him, ma'am, if you ain't spoke for. His kind run mighty scarce."

After a moment, he opened his eyes again. "You knowed that man come to my camp?"

"Colby Rafin." She was silent for a moment, and then she said, "They were looking for us, I think."

"For *him*?" he half-lifted a hand toward me. "They're crazy!"

Galloway came in out of the dark, and I whispered to him about Rafin and how the herd was lost.

"It's like them — outlaws always. Now they've turned cattle thieves."

Neither one of us had much to say, because we were both thinking the same thing. The Fetchens had come west, all right, and they had come a-hunting us. The trouble was they had us outnumbered by a good bit, and running off this herd showed they'd taken the full step from being rowdies and trouble makers to becoming genuine outlaws. From now on it would be a fight to the death against an outfit that would stop at nothing . . . and us with a girl to watch out for.

That Colorado ranch began to look mighty

far away, and I was cursing the hour when I first saw Costello or Judith.

Not that we minded a fight. We Sacketts never had much time for anything else. If we weren't fighting for our country we were fighting men who still believed in rule by the gun, and no Sackett I ever heard of had ever drawn a gun on a man except in self-defense, or in defense of his country or his honor.

Right then I was glad Galloway stood beside me. Nobody ever needed an army when they had Galloway, and maybe one other Sackett . . . it didn't make much difference which one.

Chapter 3

We hit trail before sunup, keeping off the skyline as much as possible, but always moving westward, riding sidewise in the saddle so as we could look all around, Galloway facing one way, me the other.

There was a look to the sky that spelled a weather change, but we didn't pay it no mind, figuring only to get distance behind us.

Short of noon a man came up from the south riding a paint pony and hazing about thirty head of cattle. When he put eyes on us he rode his pony around the cattle and came up to us, keeping his Winchester handy and studying us careful-like.

"You pass anybody back yonder? I'm huntin' my outfit."

The brand on his pony and those cattle spelled the story for me — a Half-Box H. "You got stampeded a while back," I said, "and one of

40

your outfit died in our camp."

"Which one?"

"Said he was the cook. Come to think on it, he never did give us his name. Said he rode for Evan Hawkes, and he told us Hawkes's boy got killed in the stampede."

The man's face showed shock. "The boy's dead? That'll go hard on the boss. He set store by the lad."

Me, I curled one leg around the pommel and pushed my hat back. "Mister, looks to me like your herd was scattered hell to breakfast. We covered some miles back yonder and seen nobody. What you figure to do?"

"Drive these cattle into Dodge an' report to Evans Hawkes. All I can do."

He told me his name was Briggs. "Might as well ride with us," I said to him. "It's one more gun for each of us."

"What's that mean?"

"That was James Black Fetchen's outfit from Tennessee who jumped your herd. They're hunting us. If we meet up with them there'll be shooting, and you can lay to it that if they see you're alive they'll be after you, too."

"I'll ride along," he said.

During the next hour we picked up thirteen head of scattered cattle wearing the Hawkes brand. By nightfall we had close to fifty head more. We'd scarcely made camp when we were hailed out of the night . . . in those days no man in his right mind rode up to a strange camp without giving them a call.

"That'll be Ladder Walker," Briggs said. "I know the voice."

Walker was an extra tall, extra lean man, which was why they called him Ladder. He was driving six head of steers, and he had a lump on his skull and a grouch over what happened. "You catch sight of any of that bunch?" he asked Briggs. "All I ask is a sight down a gun barrel at them."

"You stand easy, friend," Galloway said. "That's a mean outfit. If they can help it you'll not get a shooting chance."

The upshot of it was that of the herd of fifteen hundred cattle the Half-Box H sent up the trail, we drove into Dodge with a hundred and twenty, picked up along the way. No doubt a few more riders could have combed twice that number out of the breaks along the creeks and the coulees, scattered stuff left behind from the stampede.

Now, we Sacketts carried a name known in Dodge. Tyrel, Orrin, and some of the others had come into Dodge long before, Tyrel and Orrin being there when the town was mighty young. They were the first Sacketts to go west to settle.

42

Their pa had come west earlier than that, riding and trapping fur along with Bridger, Carson, and Joe Meek. He'd never come back from his last trip, so it was always figured that some Blackfoot had raised his hair, back up in Montana. We'd heard the story as youngsters, but had never known any of that branch of the family until we bumped into Tyrel and Orrin down in the Mogollon, where they'd gone to lend a fighting hand to their brother Tell.

Knowing that if the other riders had come through the stampede alive, they would head for Hawkes at his hotel, we went along with Walker and Briggs. Three other riders had already come in, which left seven missing.

Evan Hawkes was a tall, broad-shouldered but spare-built man with darkish red hair. The build of him and the way he combed his hair reminded a body of Andy Jackson, and he had a pair of gray eyes that advised a man he'd make a better friend than an enemy.

"They've got that herd to sell," Hawkes said, "and we will be there when they try. I'll pass the word around."

"Mr. Hawkes," I said, "you got to remember that Fetchen is no fool. From all I hear, he's mighty shrewd, as well as mean. He may not sell that herd at all."

"What do you mean?"

"From what I've seen of those we gathered, you had quite a bit of young breeding stock. Fetchen could push that herd west into Wyoming, peddle the steers to Indians or the army or some beef contractor. Then he could use the young stuff to start his own outfit."

"You believe he has come west to stay?"

"I've been wondering about that. It doesn't seem reasonable they'd all come west without reason. I figure something happened back there after we left."

Judith had been standing by getting madder by the minute, and now she let go at all of us. "You've no right to suppose anything of the kind! And you've no evidence that Black Fetchen stole that herd!"

Hawkes looked at her, kind of surprised. "It seems to be there's a difference of opinion among you."

"The little lady doesn't think Black is all that mean," Galloway said.

"I certainly do not!"

"The way we figure it," Galloway went on, "what happened to you is mostly our fault. You see, the Fetchens came west hunting us. Black wants the little lady here, and he wants her horses, some of the finest breeding stock you ever did see. Back there in Tazewell —"

"Tennessee?" said Hawkes. "I know it well.

44

I'm from Kentucky."

"Well, we had a run-in with those boys, sort of calmed 'em down when they were about to show their muscle. They been used to having things their own way."

Leaving Hawkes with his riders, the three of us went downstairs to the dining room. Judith had her nose up, and her cheeks were flushed and angry. When we'd found seats at a table she said, "You have no right to talk that way about Mr. Fetchen. He is an honorable man."

"I hope so," Galloway commented, "because if he wasn't, and you went to him, you'd be in a kind of a fix, wouldn't you? This far from home, and all."

We ordered, and then she started to look around some, and so did we. Neither me nor Galloway had been to many towns. We had seen Santa Fe, Dodge, Abilene, and Sedalia, Missouri, and both of us liked to see folks around us.

There were cattle buyers, land speculators, officers from the army post, cattle drivers, gamblers and such like around. All of them were dressed to the nines, and were looking almighty fancy. Galloway and me had taken time before coming in to brush up a little, but somehow we didn't shape up like these folks. We looked like a pair of mountain boys still, and

45

it shamed me. As soon as we got some money, I thought, we'd buy us some proper clothes.

"You been to big towns, Judith?" Galloway asked her.

"I have been to Atlanta and Nashville, and to New Orleans, Mobile, and Louisville . . . oh, lots of towns. My folks traded in all of them."

I'd had no idea she was such a traveled girl, but it followed. The Irish traders were folks that got about a good bit. There for a few minutes she forgot all about Black Fetchen and took to telling us about the big towns, and believe me, we listened to every word.

The restaurant door opened while she was talking and I turned my head. It was Black Fetchen.

He had surely changed. He wore a brand-new black broadcloth suit, a white shirt, and black tie. His boots were polished like all get out, and he carried a new black hat in his hand. His hair was all slicked down with bear grease or the like, and I'll have to admit he was a handsome sight. Tory came in behind him, with Colby Rafin and another one of their outfit known as Ira Landon.

Fetchen walked right over to our table, the others sitting down across the room with their backs to us.

"Why, Judith! How nice to see you!" Then he

46

turned to me and said, "I hope you boys carry no grudge against us. We're certainly not about to hunt trouble with you. Back there we were just a-funnin' – we didn't mean no trouble."

Judith was beaming. It made me mad to see so much sparkle in her eyes over such a no-account rascal. Me, I didn't buy that flannel-mouth talk, and he knew it. All the time he was talking I could just see the taunting in his eyes; but Judith, she was all excited and happy.

"Why, sure!" Galloway was the smooth-talking one of the two of us. "Why don't you pull up a chair and set? We'd enjoy talking a while. Maybe you could tell us something about a herd of cattle somebody stampeded and run off back down the trail."

Judith's face went white and her lips tightened up. She was both mad and scared . . . scared something was going to happen.

"Cattle? Since when did you two go into the cattle business?"

"They weren't our cattle," Galloway said as smooth as silk. "They belong to a friend of ours, name of Evan Hawkes . . . a good man. His herd was stampeded by some rustlers . . . murderers, too, because they killed his boy, and some of his men."

Fetchen never batted an eye. Oh, he was a cool one! He just smiled and said, "Come to think of it, we did see a few stray cattle. We even drove in half a dozen and turned them over to the marshal."

He pulled back a chair and sat down, easy as you please. "As a matter of fact, I didn't just come over to say howdy to some old friends from the home state. I came over to see Judith. Seems you boys aren't going to give me a chance to be alone with her, so I'll have to speak my piece right here before all of you."

Judith's eyes were shining and her lips were parted. I didn't like it to see her getting so flustered. Before I could say anything, Black Fetchen, still smiling like the cat sizing up the canary, says, "Judith, will you marry me?"

And before either of us can say aye, yes, or no, she ups and says, "Yes, James — yes, I will!"

"I'm honored, ma'am, right honored." Then he says, "I don't think it is really the right thing for a man's betrothed to be spending so much time with two men, single men who are no kin to her, so I've taken a room for you here at the hotel until we're married."

We sat there, caught flat-footed. This here was something we hadn't expected, nor did we know what to do. It was Galloway who spoke first. "That's right nice, Black," he said, "but her grandpa asked us most particular to take her to her pa in Colorado. Now, it ain't so many miles from here, so why don't you two figure on being married there where her pa can attend? After all, she's his only daughter."

Fetchen never stopped smiling. "Mr. Sackett, I wouldn't expect you to understand, but I am in love. I do not want to wait."

"Nor do I!" Judith said. "We can be married right here in Dodge."

Galloway didn't show any ire, even if he felt it. He just said, "It would be nice if your pa knew, Judith. Do you care so little for him?"

That got to her, and she sobered up, suddenly so serious I thought she might cry.

"It's a noble sacrament," I said, "and a rare thing for a man to see his daughter wedded to the man of her choice."

She looked up at Fetchen. "James . . . maybe we should wait. After all, it isn't very far."

Black's lips tightened and his eyes squinted just a mite. I'd always heard he carried a fearful temper, liable to burst out whenever he was thwarted, and it was edging toward the surface now. Maybe if she saw him in a rage it would help. Me and Galloway must have been thinking the same thing. Only trouble was, I up and made a damn fool of myself. I said the wrong thing.

"Besides," I said, "Judith is only a youngster.

49

She's not old enough to marry."

Judith ran up her flag and let go with all her guns, she was that mad. "Flagan Sackett, you wouldn't know a woman if you saw one! I am so old enough! We'll just show you how old I am! James, if you're ready we can be married tomorrow morning."

Fetchen straightened up. Of course, that was all he wanted all the time. He threw me a look that was what a body might call triumphant. "I would be honored, Judith. If you'll come with me I'll show you to your room."

Judith got up and turned her back squarely to me. I started to speak, but what could I say?

Fetchen turned and looked back at us. "Gentlemen, I'll send a couple of the boys over for my fiancée's clothing and her horses — all of them."

"What do you mean, all of them?"

"I mean those you two have been riding. They are Costello horses."

"For which we have a bill of sale," I said calmly, but I was fighting mad underneath.

"That's right, James," Judith said. "Those horses belong to them."

"We will look into that a bit further," Fetchen replied. "I do not think those bills of sales, as you call them, will stand up in court."

They walked away together and left us sitting

there, and of a sudden I no longer had any appetite. Youngster she might be, but I had no wish to see any girl in the hands of Black Fetchen.

"Galloway, we can't let him do it. We got to stop him."

"You tell me how. She wants to marry him, and we can't prove a thing against him."

"Do you suppose he really drove in some Half-Box H cattle?"

"I'd lay a bet on it. Oh, he's a smart one! If anybody saw him with cattle of that brand, he's now got himself an alibi. Also, it makes him look good with the other cattlemen around."

"What's he see in her, do you suppose?"

Galloway, he gave me an odd look. "Why, you damn' fool, that's a right pretty little girl. Shapes up like pretty much of a woman. And in case you forget, Ma was no older when she married Pa."

He was right, only I didn't like to admit it. That Judith seemed like a youngster . . . all those freckles and everything. Only when I started reminding myself of that everything, I got to remembering that what Galloway had been saying was right. She was nigh to being a woman, even if she wasn't one yet . . . in my judgment, anyway.

"Flagan, what are we going to do?"

Upshot of it was, we went to see the marshal, Wyatt Earp, but he said he could do nothing. "Sorry, boys." He was kind of abrupt. "Mr. Fetchen brought in some of the Hawkes cattle and turned them over at the corral. That certainly doesn't make him seem a thief. Also, there seems to be no evidence that he had anything to do with running off the herd. As for the girl, she is old enough to marry, and she wants to marry him. I am afraid I can do nothing."

Bat Masterson was sheriff of Ford County, and we went next to see him. He was a right handsome young man about twenty-four or -five years old, wearing a dark suit and black derby hat. You had to be quite a man to wear a hard hat in those days; it was such a temptation for some half-drunk cowpoke to try to shoot it off your head. Bat's didn't carry any bullet marks that I could see.

He listened to what we had to say, then shook his head. "Sorry, boys, there's nothing I can do. The girl has a right to marry, and there's no warrant out for any of that crowd." He paused a minute. "Although I've got some good ideas of my own."

"Anything we can tie to?" Galloway asked.

"No. But a man who rode in the other day said he saw the Fetchen outfit driving about fifty head of cattle. They didn't turn in but half a dozen scrubs."

"Ain't that evidence?"

"Not exactly. Rufe was drunk when he saw them. Now, I'd take his word for how many head he saw, drunk or sober — Rufe's an old cowhand. But I doubt if you could make it stick in a court of law."

"What can we do?"

Masterson tipped back in his chair and considered the question. "I'd say you might wire her grandfather. Get authority from him to hold up the wedding. And wire her father too."

Well now. Neither one of us had even thought of that, because we'd had no truck with telegraph wires. We'd heard about them, and seen the wires along the railroad tracks, but the idea of sending a message to Costello never occurred to us.

"If you'd write us out a message, we'd be obliged," I said, "and you'd be helping a mighty nice girl from a bad marriage."

So Bat taken up a pen and scratched out the message. I had figured a body would have to write it some special way, but nothing of the kind.

He wrote it out, slick as you please: *Fetchen here. Proposed marriage, Judith accepted. Wire authority to stop marriage.*

53

"If we get a wire from Costello saying he refuses permission," Masterson said, "I'll stop it."

When we had sent the message we stood on the boardwalk in front of the Long Branch and considered the situation. Of a sudden, Galloway had an idea. "This sort of town," he said thoughtfully, "I wonder how many preachers it's got?"

"Three, four, maybe."

He was looking at me kind of funny-like and I began to read the sign of what he was thinking. "Now, that there," I said, "is what comes of contemplating. I think we better ask around."

"Ladder Walker, Harry Briggs, and them," Galloway said, "they owe us a favor, and Hawkes told me this morning that they were holding what cattle they'd found about fifteen miles north of here. I figure one of those boys should talk to a preacher. Ladder, f'r instance. If he was dyin' he would surely want a preacher."

About that time Bat came walking down the street headed for the Long Branch, carrying the cane from which he had taken his name.

"Mr. Masterson," I said, "how many preachers in Dodge?"

Bat's eyes started to twinkle. "You're lucky," he said. "They're all out of town but one." And then he added, "Don't forget the justice of the peace."

Galloway, he rounded up his horse and headed for the camp on the run to set up the deal at that end. Me, I mounted up, taken my horse out of town for a good run, and brought him back into town and up to the preacher's house, all lathered up.

"Reverend," I said, "there's a man in a bad way out to a cow camp, and he's bound to make his peace with the Lord. Will you ride out to him?"

Now, that sky pilot was a right fine gentlemen who put down his coffee cup, wiped his mouth, and harnessed his team. I hooked up the traces whilst he slipped into his coat. In less time than it takes to tell about it, he was ready.

"One more thing," I said, "he wishes to make a will, and he said the man he wanted to draw it up for him was the justice of the peace. Said he didn't know whether the J.P. was a proper lawyer or not, but he doesn't care. He believes he's an honest man."

Well, with me riding alongside the buckboard we made it to the J.P.'s house and he was quick enough to go. It looked like a good fee and he was ready. They went dusting out of town in that buckboard, riding on their mission of mercy, and I tailed behind them.

When we rode up to the camp it was nothing

but a corral, a spring, and a sod shanty that was half dugout. Ladder Walker was a-lying on his back with a blanket pulled up over him, and he looked sicker than anybody I ever did see. Those others cowpokes were all standing around with their hats off, talking in low voices.

As soon as all was going well, Galloway and me slipped out and rode back to Dodge. It looked to me as if Ladder was shaping up to one of the longest death scenes in history.

Although the preacher said he was a Protestant, and confession was not necessary, Ladder couldn't miss a chance like that. So he started off by confessing to several hours of the most lurid sinning a body ever heard tell of. He had confessed to all he had done, which was a-plenty, all he had wanted to do, which was a sight more, and then he began inventing sins the like of which you never heard. I'll say one thing for him. He had him an audience right from the word go. They never even looked up when we went out.

"You can bet your bottom dollar," Galloway said, "they'll never get out of there tonight."

The thing that worried us, suppose one of those sky pilots who had been out of town should return?

Only they didn't.

Chapter 4

Galloway and me, we rode up to the hitch rail in front of the Lady Gay and stepped down from our saddles. We were hungry and tired, and it was coming on to storm. As we stood on the boardwalk sizing up the town, lightning flashed out over the prairie.

"Looks to be a gully-washer," Galloway said. "I've been watching those clouds all the way in."

"You go ahead. I'll put up the horses." I hesitated there a moment, then added, "You might look to see if Judith has switched her gear over to that room Fetchen got for her."

The street was empty. I could hear boots on the walk down half a block or so, but could see nobody. The saloons were all lit up, going full blast, but there were few horses or rigs around because of the storm a-coming.

Leading both horses, I walked across the street and went on down to the livery stable. On the corner I held up for a moment, watching a tumbleweed rolling down the street and thinking of that Judith. Of all the contrary, ornery, freckle-faced . . . Trouble was, I missed her.

There was a lantern over the livery stable door, the flame sputtering in the wind. Nobody was around, so I led the horses back to their stalls and tied them, then went up a ladder into the loft and forked hay down to both of them. I was finishing off the last fork of hay when I thought I heard a step down below, a slow, careful step.

The loft where I was covered the whole top of the barn, and there were three ladders up to it — three that I'd seen, two on one side, one on the other. Come to think of it, there should be a fourth ladder, but if there was it must come down in an empty stall at the back of the barn where the liveryman hung spare bits of harness, tools, and suchlike.

All the time I was thinking of that, I was listening. Had somebody followed me in? Or was it some drunk hunting a place to sleep away from the storm? Or maybe somebody coming to get his horse?

The way those footsteps sounded made me think it was surely not one of the last two. My Winchester was down there beside my saddle and my slicker, waiting to be picked up before I went to the hotel. Likely that man down there had seen them and was just a-playing 'possum, waiting for me to come down and pick them up. And whatever lead he could throw at me.

Now, some folks might think me a suspicious man, and they'd be right. Many's the time I've suspected something when I was wrong; but there were other times I'd been right, and so I was still among the living.

Slipping the rawhide thong off the hammer of my six-shooter, I put that pitchfork down as easy as I could. Then I straightened up to listen. If he knew I was up here I'd best stir a mite, or he'd be suspicious.

Many a cowpoke slept in a livery stable, and that was the idea I hoped to give him. What I figured on was getting him to come up that ladder, instead of him catching me coming down.

All the same, I started figuring. Seems to me a man can most usually take time to contemplate, and if he does it will save him a lot of riding and a lot of headaches.

Now, suppose I was down there and wanted to shoot a man on one of those ladders? Where would I take my stand so's I could watch all three to once?

It didn't leave much choice. Two ladders were on one side of the loft, opposite to him; the other ladder he knew of was on his side of the loft, up toward the front. If the man below wanted to keep all of them under cover, he had to be somewhere on the right side of the stable, toward the rear. If there was another ladder, which went up from that empty stall, one long unused, it would be behind the watcher.

If I made a try at coming down any one of the three ladders now, I'd be climbing down with my back to the gunman — if that was what he was.

The first thing I did was to sit down on some hay. I fluffed some of it around as if I was shaping a bed, and not being careful about noise; then I took off my boots and dropped them on the floor. After that I picked them up, tyed them together with a piggin string, and slung them around my neck. Then, just as carefully as I could, I stood up in my sock feet. The floor was solid and not likely to squeak, so I eased across, soundlessly as I was able. And I waited.

There was not a sound from below. Near me was a bin full of corn, unshelled corn waiting to be fed to some of the local horses. I tossed an ear of that corn over to where I had taken off my boots, and it hit the boards near the hay. I hoped he would believe I'd dropped something, or something had slipped from my pockets.

Then I eased along the side of the loft till I was over that empty stall. Sure enough, there was an opening there, with a ladder leading down.

It was well back in the stall and in a dark corner. The chances were that few of the stable's customers had any idea that this ladder was there.

Crouching by the opening, I listened, but heard no sound. I drew my Colt and carefully lowered my head until I could see into the lower level. . . . Nothing.

Swinging my feet down, my Colt gripped in my right hand, I felt for the first rung of the ladder, found it, and then the second. Lowering myself down, clinging to the ladder, I searched for him but could see nothing. I came down a step further, and heard a shout.

"Got you, damn it!" A gun blasted not over thirty feet away. The bullet smashed into the frame of the ladder, stabbing my face with splinters, and I fired in return, my bullet going slightly above and left of the flash. I realized even as I fired that my shot was too high, and I triggered a second shot lower down.

At the same instant I let go and dropped, landing on the balls of my feet, but I tumbled forward with a crash of harness and a breaking chair; and then came the bellow of a gun, almost within inches of me.

Rolling over, I fired again.

Outside I heard a shout, heard running feet, and I sprang up. Down the far side of the stalls near the horses a man was staggering. He was bent far over, clutching at his stomach, and even as I saw him he stumbled forward and fell on his face.

The running feet were coming nearer.

Ducking out the back door of the barn, I slid between the corral bars and, still in my sock feet, ran lightly along the area back of the buildings until I was close to the hotel. I paused for just a moment and got my boots on, and then I went up the back stairs of the hotel, and along the hall.

Several heads appeared from doorways, and one of them was Judith's. She saw me, and for a moment I thought I saw relief on her face. "Flagan, what is it? What's happened?" she asked.

"Some drunken cowhand," I said. "You've got to expect that in Dodge."

She still stood there in the door of her room. She was fully dressed, although it was very late. "I will be married tomorrow," she said, almost tentatively.

"I wish you luck."

"You don't really mean that."

"No, ma'am, I don't. I think you're doing the

hey had gone, I said, "Judith, I'm
t you into this."
re standing here with me!" she in-
hy, I must have come out of my door
se shots died away."
been quick enough. The trouble is
ning man can cover a good distance,
just never calculate time as well as
. In any event, she had stopped a
ting in a crowded place where she or
ght have been hurt, and for that much
d.
idn't tell the truth," she said then.
sn't going out of town. He was going
inner with James and me."
r dinner, isn't it?"
said he would be busy. He wanted to
He said the restaurant would not be so

ter go," I said. I backed off a few steps.
ange your mind, you can always come
join us. We'll take you on to your pa."
iled a little. "Flagan, I shall not
y mind. I love James, and he loves

eep telling yourself that. Maybe after a
u'll come to believe it," I said.
n Sackett, I —"
it isn't right for a gentleman to walk

wrong thing, and I know it isn't what your
grandpa wanted . . . nor your pa, either, I'm
thinking."

"Mr. Fetchen is a fine man. You'll see."

We heard voices from down below, and then
boots on the stairs. Colby Rafin was suddenly
there, Black Fetchen behind him, with Norton
Vance and Burr Fetchen coming up in the rear.

"There he is!" Colby yelled.

He grabbed for his gun, but I had him
covered. Back in Tennessee those boys never
had to work at a fast draw, and the way that
gun came into my hand stopped them
cold.

"I don't know what you boys are looking for,"
I said, "but I don't like being crowded."

"You killed Tory!" Burr shouted.

Before I could open my mouth to speak,
Judith said, "How could he? He's been standing
here talking to me!"

That stopped them, and for the moment
nobody thought to ask how long I'd been there.
After that moment they never got the chance,
because the marshal pushed by them.

"What happened down there?" he asked me.

"Sounded like some shooting. These boys say
Tory Fetchen got killed."

Just then Bat Masterson came up the steps.
"Everything all right, Wyatt?" Then he saw me

standing there at Judith's door. "Oh, hello, Sackett."

Earp turned on him. "Do you know this man, Bat?"

"Yes, I do. He brought Evan Hawkes's cattle in, and helped round up some strays. He's a friend of mine."

Earp glanced down at my boots. "Mind if I look at your boots? The man who did that shooting had to come along behind the buildings. It's muddy there."

I lifted one boot after the other. Both were as slick as though they'd never stepped on anything but a board floor.

Colby Rafin was sore. He simply couldn't believe it. "He's lyin'!" he shouted. "It had to be him! Why, Tory was —"

"Tory was what?" Masterson demanded. "Laying for him? Was that it?"

It was Burr who spoke up. "Nothin' like that," he protested, "Tory just went after his horse."

"At this hour?" Earp asked. "You mean he was riding out of town this late, with a storm brewing?"

"Sure," Burr replied easily. "He was riding out to join some of our outfit."

"Gentlemen," Earp said coldly, "before we ask any further questions or you give any more answers, let me tell you something. Your

64

Friend Tory Fetch
with a very distinc
enough tracks dowr
man who was doing
crouched down or s
support posts. From
waiting for somebod
sight. He was either r
time. In any case, his
he was hit twice . . .
shot cut the top of his
case against the man
were armed, both we
but a matter of clear

"Just a question, ge
"You came up here,
Sackett's room. Did
finishing the job Tory

"Aw, it was nothing
waved a careless han
trouble back in Tenne

"Then I suggest you
and settle it," Earp in
shooting in Dodge."

"I give you my wor
won't shoot unless I'm

"That's fair enough,
boys go about your busi
trouble I'll lock you up

When t
sorry I go
"You we
sisted. "W
just as th

She had
that a run
and folks
they thin
nasty sho
others mi
I was gla
"They
"Tory wa
to have
"Late f
"James
eat later.
crowded.
"I'd be
"If you c
back and
She s
change
me."
"You
while y
"Flaga
Maybe

6

away whilst a lady is talking, but I did. This was an argument where I was going to have the last word, anyway . . . when they found no preacher in town.

There was a corner at the head of the stairs where a body couldn't be seen from above or below, and I stopped there long enough to reload my gun.

Galloway was sitting in the lobby holding a newspaper. He looked up at me, a kind of quizzical look in his eyes. "Hear there was a shooting over to the livery," he said.

"Sounded like it," I agreed, and sat down beside him. In a low tone I added, "That Tory laid for me whilst I was putting hay down the chute. He come close to hangin' up my scalp."

"Yeah, and you better start pullin' slivers out of your face. The light's brighter down here than in that hallway upstairs."

Something had been bothering my face for several minutes, but I'd been too keyed up and too busy talking to notice it much. Gingerly, I put my hand up and touched the end of a pine sliver off that post. Two or three of them I pulled out right there, getting them with my fingers, but there were some others.

We walked down the street to the Peacock, just to look around, and Bat was there. He came over to us, glanced at the side of my face and smiled a little. "I hope you had time to change your socks," he said. "A man can catch cold with wet, muddy socks on."

Me, I had to grin. "Nothing gets by you, does it?"

"I saw you go into the barn. I also saw Tory follow you. I saw the track of a sock foot just back of the barn. I kicked straw over it."

"Thanks."

"When I take to a man, I stand by him. I have reason to believe that you're honest. I have reason to believe the Fetchens are not."

But, no matter how good things looked right at that moment, I was worried. Black Fetchen was not one to take Tory's shooting lying down, and no matter what anybody said, he would lay it to me or Galloway. I'd had no idea of killing anybody; only when a man comes laying for you, what can you do? The worst of it was, he'd outguessed me. All the time, he knew about that other door from the loft, and he figured rightly that I'd find it and use it. That he missed me at all was pure accident. I'd been mostly in the dark or he'd have hit me sure, and he'd been shooting to kill.

After a bit Galloway and me went back to the hotel and crawled into bed. But I slept with a Colt at my hand, and I know Galloway did, too.

Tomorrow two things would happen, both of

them likely to bring grief and trouble. First would be Tory's funeral, and second would be when they tried to find somebody to marry Judith and Black Fetchen.

Anybody could read a funeral sermon, but it took a Justice of the Peace or an ordained minister to marry somebody.

Chapter 5

There was a light rain falling when we went down to the restaurant for breakfast. It was early, and not many folks were about at that hour. The gray faces of the stores were darkened by the rain, and the dust was laid for a few hours at least. A rider in a rain-wet slicker went by on the street, heading for the livery stable. It was a quiet morning in Dodge.

We stopped at the dining room door, studying the people inside before we entered, and we found a table in a corner where we could watch both doors. Galloway had the rawhide thong slipped back off his six-shooter and so did I, but we were hunting no trouble.

Folks drifted in, mostly men. They were cattlemen, cattle buyers, a scattering of ranch hands, and some of the business folks from the stores. A few of them we already knew by sight, a trick that took only a few hours in Dodge.

There were half a dozen pretty salty characters in that room, too, but Dodge was full of them. As far as that goes, nine-tenths of the adult males in Dodge had fought in the War Between the States or had fought Indians, and quite a few had taken a turn at buffalo hunting. It was no place to come hunting a ruckus unless you were hitched up to go all the way.

We ordered scrambled eggs and ham, something a body didn't find too much west of the Mississippi, where everything was beef and beans. Both of us were wearing store-bought clothes and our guns were almost out of sight. There was a rule about packing guns in town unless you were riding out right off, but the law in Dodge was lenient except when the herds were coming up the trail, and this was an off season for that. Evan Hawkes had been almost the only one up the trail right at that time.

Nowhere was there any sign of the Fetchen crowd, nor of Judith.

"You don't suppose they pulled out?" Galloway asked.

" 'Tisn't likely."

Several people glanced over at us, for there were no secrets in Dodge, and by now everybody in town would know who we were and why we were in town; and they would also know the Fetchen crowd.

It was likely that Earp had figured out the shooting by this time, but as had been said, Tory was armed and it was a fair shooting, except that he laid for me like that. He'd tried to ambush me, and he got what was coming to him. Dodge understood things like that.

We ate but our minds were not on our food, hungry as we were, for every moment we were expecting the Fetchens to show up. They did not come, though. The rain eased off, although the clouds remained heavy and it was easy enough to see that the storm was not over. Water dripped from the eaves and from the signboards extending across the boardwalk in some places.

We watched through the windows, and presently a man came in, pausing at the outside door to beat the rain from his hat and to shake it off his raincoat. He came on in, and I heard him, without looking at us, tell Ben Springer, "They had their buryin'. There were nineteen men out there. Looked to be a tough lot."

"Nineteen?" Galloway whispered. "They've found some friends, seems like."

We saw them coming then, a tight riding bunch of men in black slickers and mostly black hats coming down the street through the mud. They drew up across the street and got down from their horses and went to stand under the overhang of the building across the street.

Two turned and drifted down the street to the right, and two more to the left, the rest of them stayed there. It looked as if they were waiting for us.

"Right flatterin', I call it," Galloway said, picking up his coffee cup. "They got themselves an army yonder."

"Be enough to go around," I commented. Then after a minute I said, "I wonder what happened to Judith?"

"You go see. I'll set right here and see if they want to come a-hunting. If they don't, we'll go out to 'em after a bit."

Pushing back my chair, I got up and went into the hotel and up the stairs. When I got to her door, I rapped . . . and rapped again.

There was no answer.

I tried rapping again, somewhat louder, and when no answer came I just reached down and opened the door.

The room was empty. The bed was still unmade after she'd slept in it, but she was gone, and her clothes were gone.

When I came back down the stairs I came down moving mighty easy. Nothing like walking wary when a body is facing up to trouble, and I could fairly smell trouble all around.

Nobody was in the lobby, so I walked over to

where I could see through the arch into the dining room.

Galloway was sitting right where I'd left him, only there were two Fetchens across the table from him and another at the street door, and all of them had guns.

The tables were nigh to empty. Chalk Beeson was sitting across the room at a table with Bob Wright; and Doc Halliday, up early for him, was alone at another table, drinking his breakfast, but keeping an eye on what was happening around.

Black Fetchen was there, along with Burr and a strange rider I didn't know, a man with a shock of hair the color of dead prairie grass, and a scar on his jaw. His heels were run down, but the way he wore his gun sized him up to be a slick one with a shootin' iron, or one who fancied himself so. A lot of the boys who could really handle guns wore them every which way, not slung down low like some of the would-be fast ones.

"It was your doing," Black was saying, "you and that brother of yours. You got that preacher out of town. Well, it ain't going to do you no good. Judith is ridin' west with us, and we'll find us a preacher."

"I'd not like to see harm come to that girl," Galloway commented calmly. "If harm comes to her I'll see this country runs mighty short on Fetchens."

"You won't have the chance. You ain't going to leave this room. Not alive, you ain't."

About that time I heard a board creak. It was almost behind me, and it was faint, but I heard it. Making no move, I let my eyes slant back. Well, the way the morning sunlight fell through the window showed a faint shadow, and I could just see the toe of a boot — a left boot.

Just as I sighted it, the toe bent just a mite like a man taking a step or swinging a gun to hit a man on the head. So I stepped quickly off to the right and back-handed my left fist, swinging hard.

When he cut down with that six-gun barrel he swung down and left, but too slow. My left fist smashed him right in the solar plexus, right under the third button of his shirt, and the wind went out of him as if he'd been steer-kicked. His gun barrel came down, his blow wasted, and by that time my right was moving. It swung hard, catching him full in his unprotected face, smashing his nose like a man stepping on a gourd.

The blood gushed out of his nose and he staggered back, and I walked in on him.

Now, there's a thing about fighting when the chips are down. You get a man going, you don't let up on him. He's apt to come back and beat your ears down. So I reached out, caught him by one ear and swung another right, scattering a few of his teeth. He turned sidewise, and I drove my fist down on his kidney like a hammer, and he hit the floor.

Now, that all amounted to no more than four or five seconds. A body doesn't waste time between punches, and I wasn't in anything less than a hurry.

Nor was I making much noise. It was all short and sharp and over in an instant, and then I was facing back toward that room.

Galloway was sitting easy. Nobody ever did fluster that boy. He was a soft-talking man, but he was tough, and so rough he wore out his clothes from the inside first. There were Fetchens ready to fire, but Galloway wasn't worried so's a body could see, and I was half a mind to leave it all to him. It would serve them right.

One time when he was short of thirteen we were up in the hills. We'd been hunting squirrels and the like, but really looking for a good razor-back hog, Ma being fresh out of side-meat. Well, Galloway seen a big old boar back under the brush, just a-staring at him out of those mean little eyes, and Galloway up and let blast at him. That bullet glanced off the side of the boar's shoulder and the hog took off into the brush. We trailed him for nigh onto two miles before he dropped, and when we came upon him there was a big old cougar standing over him.

Now, that cougar was hungry and he'd found meat, and he wasn't figuring on giving up to no mountain boy. Galloway, he'd shot that wild boar and we needed the side-meat, and he wasn't about to give it up to that big cat. So there they stood, a-staring one at the other.

Galloway was carrying one load in that old smooth-bore he had, and he knew if he didn't get the cat with one shot he would be in more trouble than he'd ever seen. A wounded cougar is something nobody wants any truck with, but if that cougar'd known who he was facing he'd have taken out running over the hills.

Galloway up and let blast with his gun just as that cougar leaped at him. The bullet caught the cat in the chest but he was far-off from dead. He knocked Galloway a-rolling and I scrambled for a club, but Galloway was up as quick as the cougar, and he swung the smooth-bore and caught that cat coming in, with a blow on the side of the head. Then before the stunned cougar could more than get his feet under him, Galloway outs with his Arkansas toothpick and then he and that cat were going around and around.

Blood and fur and buckskin were flying every which way, and then Galloway was up and bleeding but that cat just lay there. He looked at Galloway and then just gave up the ghost right there before us.

Galloway had his ribs raked and he carries the cougar scars to this day. But we skinned out the cougar and toted the hide and the side-meat home. We made shift to patch Galloway up, and only did that after he lay half naked in a cold mountain stream for a few minutes.

What I mean is, Galloway was nobody to tackle head-on without you figured to lose some hide.

Galloway, he just sat there a-looking at them, that long, tall mountain boy with the wide shoulders and the big hands. We two are so much alike we might be twins, although we aren't, and he's away the best-looking of the two. Only I can almost tell what he's thinking any given time. And right then I wouldn't have wanted to be in the shoes of any Fetchen.

"I'm going to leave this room, Fetchen," he said, "and when I please to. If I have to walk over Fetchens I can do it. I figure you boys are better in a gang or in a dark barn, anyway."

Black came to his feet as if he'd been stabbed with a hat pin. "It was you, was it?"

"Don't push your luck." Galloway spoke easy

enough. "The only reason you're alive now is because I don't figure it polite to mess up a nice floor like this. Now, if I was you boys I'd back up and get out of here while the getting is good. And mind what I said, if one hair of that girl's head is so much as worried, I'll see the lot of you hang."

Well, they couldn't figure him. Not one of them could believe he would talk like that without plenty of guns to back him. He was alone, it seemed like, and he was telling them where to get off, and instead of riding right over him, they were worried. They figured he had some sort of an ace-in-the-hole.

Burr glanced around and he saw me standing back from the door, but on their flank and within easy gun-range – point-blank range, that is. I was no more than twenty or twenty-five feet away, and there was nothing between us. Not one of them was facing me. For all they knew, there might be others, for they'd seen us around with some of the Half-Box H outfit.

Black got up, moving easy-like, and I'll give it to him, the man was graceful as a cat. He was a big man, too, bigger than either Galloway or me, and it was said back in the hills that in a street fight he was a man-killer.

"We can wait," he said. "We've got all the time in the world. And the first preacher we come upon west of here, Judith and me will get married."

They went out in a bunch, the way they came in, and then I strolled over from the door. Galloway glanced up. "You have any trouble?"

"Not to speak of," I said.

We walked out on the street, quiet at this hour. Somewhere a chicken had laid an egg and was telling the town about it. A lazy-looking dog trotted across the street, and somewhere a pump was working, squeaking and complaining – then I heard water gush into a pail.

A few horses stood along the street, and a freight wagon was being loaded. Right then I was thinking of none of these things, but of Judith. It seemed there was no way I could interfere without bringing on a shooting. She'd consented to marry James Black Fetchen, and we'd had no word from her folks against it. The law couldn't intervene, nor could we, but I dearly wished to and so did Galloway.

We knew there'd be more said about Tory Fetchen. That was no closed book. The Fetchens were too canny to get embroiled in a gun battle with the law when the law is such folks as Wyatt Earp, Bat Masterson, and their like. West of us the plains were wide, and what happened out yonder was nobody's business but theirs and ours. We all knew that west of here there'd be a hard reckoning some day.

We saw them coming, riding slow up the street in that tight bunch they held to, Judith out in front, riding head up and eyes straight ahead, riding right out of town and out of our lives, and they never turned a head to look at us, just rode on by like a pay car passing a tramp. They simply paid us no mind, not even Judith.

She might at least have waved good-bye.

When they disappeared we turned around and walked back inside. "Let's have some coffee," Galloway said gloomily. "We got to contemplate."

We'd no more than sat down before Evan Hawkes came in. As soon as he spotted us he walked over.

"Have you boys made any plans? If not, I can use you."

He pulled a chair around and straddled it. "If we are correct in assuming that the Fetchen crowd stampeded and stole my cattle, it seems to me they will be joining the herd somewhere west of here. No cattle have been sold that we know of, beyond a possibility of some slaughtered beef at Fort Dodge. We now have about three hundred head rounded up that I was planning on pushing to Wyoming, but I mean to have my herd back."

"How?"

"Why not the same way they got it?"

Well, why not? Fetchen had stolen his herd, so why not steal it back? There was sense to that, for nobody wants to have nigh onto fifty thousand dollars' worth of cattle taken from under his nose.

"We're riding west," I told him. "We figured to sort of perambulate around and see they treat that girl all right."

"Good! Then you boys are on the payroll as of now — thirty a month and food."

He sat there while we finished our coffee. "You boys know the Fetchens better than I do. Tell me, do they know anything about the cattle business? I mean *western* cattle business?"

"Can't see how they could. They're hill folk, like we were until we came west the first time. Howsoever, they might have some boys along who do know something . . . if they dare show their faces."

"What's that mean?"

"I figure they've tied in with some rustlers."

"That's possible, of course. Well, what do you say?"

Me, I looked at Galloway, but he left such things to me most of the time. "We're riding west, and we'd find the company agreeable," I said. "You've hired yourself some hands."

We moved out at daybreak, Evan Hawkes

riding point, and ten good men, including us. He had Harry Briggs and Ladder Walker along, and some of the others. A few, who were married men or were homesick for Texas, he paid off there. In our outfit there were, among others, two who looked like sure-fire gunmen, Larnie Cagle was nineteen and walked as if he was two-thirds cougar. The other was an older, quieter man named Kyle Shore.

Wanting to have our own outfit, Galloway and me bought a couple of pack horses from Bob Wright, who had taken them on a deal. Both were mustangs, used to making do off prairie grass, but broken to saddle and pack. Evan Hawkes was his own foreman, and I'll say this for him: he laid in a stock of grub the like of which I never did see on a cow outfit.

He had a good, salty remuda, mostly Texas horses, small but game, and able to live off the range the way a good stock horse should in that country.

The outfit was all ready to move when we reached the soddy where his boys had been holed up, so we never stopped moving.

Hawkes dropped back to me. "Flagan, I hear you're pretty good on the trail. Do you think you could pick up that outfit?"

"I can try."

There were still clouds and the weather was

threatening. A little gusty wind kept picking up, and the prairie was wet without being soggy. Galloway stayed with the herd and I cut out, riding off to the south to swing a big circle and see what I could pick up.

Within the next hour I had their sign, and by the time a second hour had gone by I had pegged most of their horses. I knew which one Judith rode and the tracks of all her other horses, and I also knew which one was Black Fetchen's. It had taken me no time at all to identify them.

This was wide-open country, and a body had to hang back a mite. Of course, they were well ahead of me, so it was not a worrisome thing right away, but it was something to keep in mind. Of course, a man riding western country just naturally looks at it all. I mean he studies his back trail and off to the horizon on every side. Years later he would be able to describe every mile of it. As if it had been yesterday.

First place, it just naturally had to be that way. There were no signposts, no buildings, no corrals, or anything but creeks, occasional buttes, sometimes a bluff or a bank, and a scatter of trees and brush. As there wasn't much to see, you came to remember what there was. And I was studying their sign because I might have to trail the whole outfit by one or two tracks.

There was one gent in that outfit who kept pulling off to one side. He'd stop now and again to study his back trail, plainly seen by the marks of his horse's hoofs in the sod. It came to me that maybe it was that new rider with the scar on his jaw. Sure enough, I came upon a place where he'd swung down to tighten his cinch. His tracks were there on the ground, run-down heels and all. Something about it smelled of trouble, and I had me an idea this one was pure poison.

And so it turned out . . . but that was another day, and farther along the trail.

Chapter 6

The land lay wide before us. We moved westward with only the wind beside us, and we rode easy in the saddle with eyes reaching out over the country, reading every movement and every change of shadow.

Now and again Galloway rode out and took the trail and I stayed with the herd, taking my turn at bringing up the drag and eating my share of dust. It was a job nobody liked, and I didn't want those boys to think I was forever dodging it, riding off on the trail of the Fetchens.

Of a noon, Galloway rode in. He squatted on his heels with those boys and me, eating a mite, drinking coffee, then wiping his hands on a handful of pulled brown grass. "Flagan," he said, "I've lost the trail."

They all looked up at him, Larnie Cagle longest of all.

"Dropped right off the world," Galloway said, "all of a sudden, they did."

"I'll ride out with you."

"Want some help?" Larnie Cagle asked. "I can read sign."

Galloway never so much as turned his head. "Flagan will look. Nobody can track better than him. He can trail a trout up a stream through muddy water."

"I got to see it," Cagle said, and for a minute there things were kind of quiet.

"Some day you might," I said.

We rode out from the herd and picked up the trail of that morning. It was plain enough, for an outfit of nineteen men and pack horses leaves a scar on the prairie that will last for a few days — sometimes for weeks.

Of a sudden they had circled and built a fire for nooning, but when they rode away from that fire there wasn't nineteen of them any longer. The most tracks we could make out were of six horses. We had trouble with the six and it wasn't more than a mile or two further on until there were only three horses ridden side by side. And then there were only two . . . and then they were gone.

It made no kind of sense. Nineteen men and horses don't drop off the edge of the world like that.

In a little while Hawkes rode over with Kyle Shore. Shore could read sign. Right away he began casting about, but he came up with nothing.

"The way I figure it, Mr. Hawkes," I said, "those boys were getting nigh to where they were going, or maybe just to those stolen cattle, so they had it in their mind to disappear. Somebody in that lot is almighty smart in the head."

"How do you think they did it?" Shore asked.

"I got me an idea," I said. "I think they bound up their horses' hoofs with sacking. It leaves no definite print, but just sort of smudges ground and grass. Then they just cut out, one at a time, each taking a different route. They'll meet somewhere miles from here."

"It's an Apache trick," Galloway said.

"Then we must try to find out where they would be apt to go," Hawkes suggested.

"Or just ride on to where they'll likely take that herd," Shore added. "Maybe we shouldn't waste time trying to follow them."

"That makes sense," I agreed.

"Suppose they just hole up somewhere out on the plains? Is there any reason why they should go farther?"

"I figure they're heading for Colorado," I said. "I think they're going to find Judith's pa."

They all looked at me, probably figuring I had Judith too much in mind, and so I did, but not this time.

"Look at it," I said. "Costello has been out there several years. He has him a nice outfit, that's why he wanted Judith with him. What's to stop them taking her on out there and just moving in on him?"

"What about him? What about his hands?"

"How many would he have on a working ranch? Unless he's running a lot of cattle over a lot of country he might not have more than four or five cowboys."

They studied about it, and could see it made a kind of sense. We had no way of telling, of course, for Fetchen might decide to stay as far from Judith's pa as possible. On the other hand, he was a wild and lawless man with respect for nothing, and he might decide just to move in on Judith's pa. It would be a good hide-out for his own herd, and unless Costello had some salty hands around, they might even take over the outfit.

Or they might do as Hawkes suggested and find a good water hole and simply stay there. In such a wide-open country there would be plenty of places.

The more I contemplated the situation the more worried I became, and I'm not usually a worrying man. What bothered me was Judith. That girl may have been a fool about James Black Fetchen; but she was, I had to admit, a smart youngster. I had an idea that, given time and company of the man and his kin, she'd come to know what he was really like. The more so since he would think he had everything in hand and under control.

What would happen if she should all of a sudden decide she was no longer inclined to marry Black Fetchen?

If she could keep her mouth shut she might get a chance to cut and run; but she was young, and liable to talk when she should be listening. Once she let Black know where he stood with her, the wraps would be off. She would have to cut and run, or be in for rough treatment.

"They don't want to be found," I told Hawkes. "They've buried the ashes of their fires. And I trailed out two of them today, lost both trails."

"What do you figure we can do?"

"Let me have Galloway, Shore, and maybe one or two others. You've got hands enough. Each one of us will work out a different trail. Maybe we can come up with something."

"You mean if the trails begin to converge? Or point toward something?"

"Sooner or later they've got to."

So it boiled down to me an' Galloway, Shore,

Ladder Walker, and an old buffalo hunter named Moss Reardon. We hunted down trails and started following them out. They were hard enough to locate in the first place.

The idea didn't pan out much. By the end of two days Walker's trail petered out in a bunch of sand hills south of us. Galloway lost his trail in the bed of a river, and Shore's just faded out somewhere on the flat. Only Reardon and me had come up with anything, and that was almighty little. Both of us lost the trail, then found it again.

When we'd joined up again with the others, I drew on the ground with a bit of stick and tried to point out what I'd found. "Right about here — and there was no trail, mind you — I found a place where the grass was cropped by a horse. It's short grass country, but the horse had cropped around in a circle, so figuring on that idea and just to prove out what I'd found, I located the peg-hole that horse had been tied to. It had been filled up, and a piece of grass tucked into the hole — growing grass."

Hawkes sort of looked at me as if he didn't believe it.

"Only there wasn't one of them, there were three. I sort of skirted around, looking for another cropped place and I found two more, further out from camp."

"You found their *camp?*"

"Such as it was. They'd dug out a block of sod, built their coffee fire in the hole, then replaced the sod when they got ready to move."

Hawkes sat back on his heels and reached for the coffeepot. He studied the map I had drawn, and I could see he was thinking about all we had learned.

"What do you think, Moss? You've hunted buffalo all over this country."

"Sand Creek," he said, "or maybe Two Buttes."

"Or the breaks of the Cimarron," Kyle Shore suggested.

Moss Reardon threw him a glance. "Now, that might be," he said. "It just might be."

We moved westward with the first light, keeping the small herd moving at a good pace. As for me, just knowing that Judith was out there ahead of us gave me an odd feeling of nearness. Up to now we hadn't been exactly certain which way she was taking, but now I had the feeling that if I was setting out to do it I could come up to them by sundown.

That night we camped on the north fork of the Cimarron, and scarcely had coffee boiling when a rider hailed the fire. In those days, as I've said before, nobody just rode up out of the dark. If he wanted to live to see grandchildren he learned to stop off a piece and call out.

When he was squatting by the fire and the usual opening talk was over, such as how did he find the grass, and how beef prices were, or had he seen any buffalo, he looked across the fire at me and said, "You'll be Flagan Sackett?"

"That I am."

"Message for you, from Bat Masterson."

He handed me a folded paper. Opening it, I found another inside.

The first was a note from Bat: *If we had known this!*

The second was an answer to our telegram sent to Tazewell: *J. B. Fetchen, Colby Rafin, Burr Fetchen and three John Does wanted for murder of Laban Costello. Apprehend and hold.*

"So they killed him," Galloway said. "I had a thought it might be so."

"We got to get that girl away from them, Galloway," I said.

"If what you surmise is true," Hawkes said, "they might want her for a bargaining point with the old man. Look at it this way. They've got a big herd of cattle and no range. They could settle on free range most anywhere, but there will be questions asked. Mine is a known brand, so if they haven't altered it, they must."

"They ain't had the time," Walker said. "Takes a spell to rope and brand that many head."

"We're wastin' time," Larnie said. "Let's locate the herd and take it from them."

"There's nineteen of them," Briggs objected. "Taking a herd from such an outfit wouldn't be that easy. A man's got to be smart to bring it off."

"Larnie's right about one thing," Hawkes said. "We've got to find the herd."

In a wide-open land like this where law was a local thing and no officer wanted to spread himself any further than his own district, a man could do just about what he was big enough to do, or that he was fast enough with a gun to do. The only restraint there was on any man outside of the settled communities was his own moral outlook and the strength of the men with him.

Black Fetchen and his kin had always ruled their roost about as they wanted, and had ridden rough-shod over those about them, but they had been kind of cornered by the country back there and the fact that there were some others around that were just as tough as they were.

The killing of Laban Costello had made outlaws of them and they had come west, no doubt feeling they'd have things their own way out here. They started off by stealing Hawkes's herd, killing his son, and some of his men as well, and seeming to get away with it.

They had been mighty shrewd about leaving no tracks. Galloway and me were good men on a trail, and without us Hawkes might never have been on to them. That's not to say that Kyle Shore and Moss Reardon weren't good — they were.

But the West Fetchen and his men were heading for wasn't quite what it had been a few years before, and I had an idea they were in for a surprise. Circumstances can change in a mighty short time where the country is growing, and the West they had heard about was, for the most of it, already gone.

For instance, out around Denver a man named Dave Cook had gotten a lot of the law officers to working together, so that a man could no longer just run off to a nearby town to be safe. And the men who rode for the law in most western towns were men who weren't scared easy.

James Black Fetchen was accounted a mighty mean man, and that passel of no-goods who rode with him could have been no better. I had an idea they were riding rough-shod for grief, because folks in Wyoming and Colorado didn't take much pushing. It's in their nature to dig in their heels and push back.

This was an uncomplicated country, as a new

country usually is. Folks had feelings and ideas that were pretty basic, pretty down to earth, and they had no time to worry about themselves or their motives. It was a big, wide, empty country and a man couldn't hide easy. There were few people, and those few soon came to know about each other. Folks who have something to hide usually head for big cities, crowded places where they can lose themselves among the many. In open western country a man stood out too much.

If he was a dangerous man, everybody knew it sooner or later; and if he was a liar or a coward that soon was known and he couldn't do much of anything. If he was honest and nervy, it didn't take long for him to have friends and a reputation for square-dealing; he could step into some big deals with no more capital than his reputation. Everybody banked on the man himself.

Once away from a town, a man rode with a gun at hand. There were Indians about, some of them always ready to take a scalp, and even the Indians accounted friendly might not be if they found a white man alone and some young buck was building a reputation to sing about when he went courting or stood tall in the tribal councils.

A rustler, if caught in the act, was usually

hung to the nearest tree. Nobody had time to ride a hundred miles to a court house or to go back for the trial, and there were many officers who preferred it that way.

Now, me and Galloway were poor folks. We had come west the first time to earn money to pay off Pa's debts, and now we were back again, trying to make our own way. And the telegram from Tennessee had changed everything.

We had made no fight when Black Fetchen claimed Judith, because she had said she was going to marry him, and we had no legal standing in the matter. But the fact that he had killed her grandpa changed everything, and we knew she'd never marry him now, not of her own free will.

"We got to get her away from them, Flagan," Galloway said, "and time's a-wasting."

But things weren't the way we would like to have them around the outfit, either. That Larnie Cagle was edgy around us. He had heard of the Sackett reputation, and he reckoned himself as good with a gun as any man; we both could see he was fairly itching to prove it.

Kyle Shore tried to slow him down, for Kyle was a salty customer and he could read the sign right. He knew that anybody who called a showdown to a Sackett was bound to get it, and

Shore being a saddle partner of Cagle's, he wanted no trouble.

Half a dozen times around camp Larnie had made comments that we didn't take to, but we weren't quarrelsome folks. Maybe I was more so than Galloway, but so far I'd sat tight and kept my mouth shut. Larnie was a man with swagger. He wanted to make big tracks, and now he had a feeling that he wasn't making quite the impression he wanted. A body could see him working up to a killing. The only question was who it would be.

Like a lot of things in this world, it was patience that finally did it for us. Galloway and me were riding out with Moss Reardon. We had followed a faint trail, picking up where we'd left off the day before, as it had run along in the same direction we were taking. On that morning, though, it veered off, doubled back, turned at right angles, switching so often it kept Galloway and me a-working at it.

All of a sudden we noticed Moss. He was off some distance across the country but we recognized that paint pony he was riding; we hung to our trail, though, and so did he. And then pretty soon we found ourselves riding together again.

"I think we've got 'em," Moss said. "As I recall, there's a hole in the river yonder where water stays on after the rest dries up. There'd be enough after a rain to water the herd."

We left the trail and took to low ground, keeping off the sky line but staying in the same direction the trail was taking. Every now and again one of us would ride out to see if we could pick up track, and sure enough, we could.

Moss Reardon's bronc began to act up. "Smells water," he said grimly. "We better ride easy."

We began to see where the grass was grazed off in the bottoms along the river. Somebody had moved a big bunch of cattle, keeping them strung out in the bottoms, which no real cattleman would do because of the trouble of working them out of the brush all the while. Only a man whose main idea was to keep a herd from view might try that.

We found a place in the river bed where there had been water, all trampled to mud by the herd, but now the water had started to seep back. We pulled up and watered our horses.

"How far do you figure?" Galloway asked.

Reardon thought a minute or two. "Not far . . . maybe three, four miles."

"Maybe one of us ought to go back and warn Hawkes."

It was coming on to sundown, and our outfit

was a good ten miles back. Nobody moved. After the horses had satisfied themselves we pulled out.

"Well" — I hooked a leg around the saddlehorn — "I figure to Injun up to that layout and see how Judith is getting along. If she's in trouble, I calculate it would be time to snake her out of there."

"Wouldn't do any harm to shake 'em up a mite," Moss suggested, his hard old eyes sharpening. "Might even run off a few head."

We swung down right there and unsaddled to rest our horses giving them a chance to graze a little. Meanwhile we sort of talked about what we might do, always realizing we would have to look the situation over before we could decide. The general idea was that we would Injun up to their camp after things settled down and scout around. If the layout looked good we might try to get Judith away; but if not, we'd just stampede that herd, or a piece of it, and drive them over to join up with the Hawkes outfit.

All the while we weren't fooling anybody. That outfit had acted mighty skittish, and they might be lying out for us. They had men enough to keep a good guard all the while, and still get what sleep they needed.

After a while we stretched out to catch ourselves a few minutes of sleep. Actually, that few minutes stretched to a good two hours, for we were beat.

Me, I was the first one up, as I am in most any camp. There was no question of starting a fire, for some of their boys might be scouting well out from camp.

I saddled up and then shook the others awake. Old Moss came out of it the way any old Indian fighter would, waking up with eyes wide open right off, and listening.

We mounted up and started off, riding easy under the stars, each of us knowing this might be our last ride. Lightly as we talked of what we might do, we knew we might be riding right into a belly full of lead.

It was near to midnight when we smelled their smoke, and a few minutes later when we saw the red glow of their fire. We could make out the figure of a man sitting on guard, the thin line of his rifle making a long shadow.

Chapter 7

We had come up to their camp from down wind so the horses wouldn't get wind of us. The cattle were bedded on a wide bench a few feet above the river, most of them lying down, but a few restless ones still grazing here and there.

There would be other guards, we knew, and without doubt one was somewhere near us even now, but we sat our horses, contemplating the situation.

About midnight those cattle would rise up, stretch, turn around a few times and maybe graze for a few minutes, and then they would lie down again. That would be a good time to start them.

We figured to start the stampede so as to run the cattle north toward our boys, which would take it right through the camp Fetchen had made, or maybe just past it. And that meant that we had to get Judith out of there before the cattle started running.

The upshot of it was that I cut off from the others and swung wide, working toward the camp. I could see the red eye of the dying fire all the while. Finally, I tied my horse in a little hollow surrounded by brush. It was a place where nobody was likely to stumble on the horse, yet I could find it quickly if I had to cut and run.

Leaving my rifle on the saddle, I started out with a six-shooter, a spare six-gun stuck down in my pants, and a Bowie knife. Switching boots for moccasins, which I carried in my saddlebags, I started easing through the brush and trees toward the camp.

Now, moving up on a camp of woods-wise mountain boys is not an easy thing. A wild animal is not likely to step on a twig or branch out in the trees and brush. Only a man, or sometimes a horse or cow, will do that, but usually when a branch cracks somewhere it is a man moving, and every man in that camp would know it.

Another distinctive sound is the brushing of a branch on rough clothing. It makes a whisking-whispering sound the ear can pick up. And as for smells, a man used to living in wild country is as keenly aware of smells as any wild creature is. The wind, too, made small sounds and, drawing near to the camp, I tried to move with the wind and to make no sudden clear sound.

The guard near the fire could be seen faintly through the leaves, and it took me almost half an hour to cover the last sixty feet. The guard was smoking a corncob pipe and was having trouble keeping it alight. From time to time he squatted near the fire, lifting twigs to relight his pipe, and that gave me an advantage. With his eyes accustomed to the glow of the fire, his sight would be poor when he looked out into the darkness.

The camp was simple enough. Men were rolled up here and there, and off to one side I could see Judith lying in the space between Black Fetchen and Burr. At her head was the trunk of a big old cottonwood, and Fetchen lay about ten feet to one side, Burr the same distance on the other. Her feet were toward the fire, which was a good twenty feet away.

There was no way to get her without stepping over one of those men, or else somehow getting around that tree trunk. Unless . . . unless the stampede started everybody moving and for the moment they forgot about her.

It was a mighty big gamble. But I thought how out on the plains a man's first thought is his horse, and if those horses started moving, or if the cattle started and the men jumped for their horses, there might be a minute or so when Judith was forgotten. If, at that moment, I was behind that tree trunk . . .

We had made no plans for such a thing, but I figured that our boys would take it for granted that I'd gotten Judith, so they would start the stampede after a few minutes. The best thing I could do would be to slip around and get back of that tree trunk, so I eased back from where I was, and when deep enough into the woods I started to circle about the camp.

But I was uneasy. It seemed to me there was something wrong, like maybe somebody was watching me, or laying for me. It was a bad feeling to have. I couldn't see anybody or hear anything, but at the same time I wasn't low-rating those Fetchen boys. I knew enough about them to be wary. They were such a tricky lot, and all of them had done their share of hunting and fighting.

When I was halfway to where I was going I eased up and stayed quiet for a spell, just listening. After a while, hearing no sound that seemed wrong, I started circling again. It took me a while, and I was getting scared they'd start those cattle moving before I could get back of that tree trunk.

Of a sudden, I heard a noise. Somebody had come into their camp. By that time I was right in line with the tree trunk, so I snaked along the ground under the brush and worked my way up behind it.

I could see Black Fetchen standing by the fire, and Burr was there too. There were three or four others with them, and they were all talking together in low tones. Something had happened . . . maybe they had seen the boys, or maybe some of their lot had seen our outfit off to the north.

About that time I saw Judith. She was lying still; her eyes were wide open and her head was tilted back a mite and she was looking right at me.

"Flagan Sackett," she whispered, "you go right away from here. If they find you they will kill you."

"I came for you."

"You're a fool. I am going to marry James Black Fetchen."

"Over my dead body."

"You stay here, and that's the way it will be. You go away."

Was I mistaken, or did she sound less positive about that business of marrying Black? Anyway, it was now or never.

I had no idea whether anything had gone wrong or not, but that stampede should have begun before this. It was unlikely I'd ever get this close again without getting myself killed, so I said, "Judith, you slip back here. Quiet now."

"I will do no such thing!"

"Judith," I said, for time was slipping away and I'd little of it left, "why do you think the whole Fetchen outfit came west?"

"They came after me!" she said proudly.

"Maybe . . . but they had another reason, too. They ran because the law wants them for murder!"

The Fetchen boys were still standing together, talking. Another man had gotten up from his blankets and gone over to join them. About that time one of the group happened to move and I saw why they were all so busy.

Standing in the center was someone who didn't belong with them, but someone who looked familiar. He turned suddenly and walked off toward his horse. I couldn't see his face, but I knew that walk. It was Larnie Cagle.

"I don't believe you!" Judith whispered.

Me, I was almighty scared. If Cagle was talking to them he would have told them we were close by, for from the way they welcomed him you'd have thought he was one of the family.

"I've got no more time to waste. Black Fetchen, Burr, and them killed your grandpa, and

I've got a telegram from Tazewell to prove it."

She gasped and started to speak; then suddenly she slipped out of her blankets, caught up her boots, and came into the brush. And I'll give her that much. When she decided to move she wasted no time, and she made no noise. She came off the ground with no more sound than a bird, and she slid between the leaves of the brush like a ghost.

We scrambled, fear crawling into my throat at being scrooched down in that brush. Suddenly behind us somebody yelled, "Judith! . . . Where's that fool girl?"

Behind us I heard them coming, and we got to our feet and started to run. Just at that moment there was a thunder of hoofs, a wild yell, a shot; then a series of yells and shots and we heard the herd start.

Glancing over my shoulder to get my direction from their fire, I could see the clearing where they were camped. Everybody had stopped dead in their tracks at those yells, and even as I looked they ran for their horses. And then the cattle hit the brush in a solid wall of plunging bodies, horns, and hoofs, . . . maddened, smashing everything down before them.

My horse was safely out of line, but we had no chance to reach him. I jumped, caught the low branch of a cottonwood and hauled myself up, then reached and grabbed Judith, pulling her up just as a huge brindle steer smashed through beneath me, flames from the fire lighting his side.

Behind us at the camp there were shots and yells as they tried to turn the herd, then I heard a scream, torn right from the guts of somebody trampled down under churning hoofs. Then the cattle were sweeping by under us, and I could feel the heat of their bodies as they smashed through.

It could have been only a few minutes, but it seemed a good deal longer than that.

As the last ones went by, I dropped to the ground, caught Judith by the hand, and she jumped down beside me. We ran over the mashed-down brush where the cattle had passed. Running, it taken us no time at all to reach my horse, and he was almightly glad to see me. I swung up, and took Judith with me on the saddle. She clung to me, arms around my waist, as I hit out for our camp where we'd planned to meet.

Yet all I could think of at the moment was Larnie Cagle. He had sold us out.

It was nigh on to daylight when I met Moss and Galloway. They came riding up, leading one of the Costello mares and a pinto pony.

Judith switched to the mare's saddle and we headed north for Hawkes's camp, rounding up what cattle we saw as we rode. By the time we reached the camp we had at least five hundred head ahead of us. The four of us had spread out, sweeping them together and into a tight bunch. Here and there as we rode, other cattle came out of the gray light of morning to join the herd.

Kyle Shore was the first man out to meet us, and right behind him came Ladder Walker.

I looked over at Shore, measuring him, and wondering if he had sold us out too. Or how far he would go to back his partner.

We walked the cattle up to the camp. Evan Hawkes, in his shirtsleeves and riding bareback, came to meet us, too.

He glanced from the cattle to Judith. What he said was, "You boys all right?"

"Yeah," I said. "But the Fetchens may be hurting. The stampede went right through their camp."

"Serves them right," Walker said.

The cattle we'd brought moved in with our herd, and we swung our horses to the fire. When I got down I stood back from the fire where I could see them all. "Who's with the herd?" I asked.

"Cagle, Bryan, and McKirdy. Briggs just

rode in to build up the cook fire."

"You sure?"

They looked at me then, they all looked at me. "Anybody seen them?" I asked.

Briggs looked around from the fire. "Everybody's all right, if that's what you mean."

"Did you talk to any of them, Briggs?"

"Sure. Dan McKirdy and me passed by several times. What are you getting at?"

There was a sound of singing then, and Larnie Cagle rode in. "How about some coffee?" he said. "I'll never make no kind of a night hawk."

I stepped forward, feeling all cold and empty inside. "I don't know about that," I said. "You did a lot of riding tonight."

Of a sudden it was so still you could almost hear the clouds passing over.

He came around on me, facing me across the fire. Nobody said anything for a moment, and when one of them spoke it was Kyle Shore.

Even before he spoke I knew what he would say, for I knew other men who had ridden other trails, men like Shore who were true to what they believed, wrong-headed though it might be.

"Larnie Cagle is a friend of mine," he said.

"Ask him where he was tonight, and then decide if he is still your friend."

"You're talking," Cagle said. "Better make it good."

"Before we start talking," I said, "let every man hold a gun. The Fetchens are coming for us, and they know right where we are. They should be here almost any minute."

Harry Briggs turned suddenly from the group. "I'll tell Dan and the boys," he said, and was gone.

Kyle Shore had been looking at me, only now he was turning his eyes upon Cagle. "What's he mean, Larnie?"

"He's talkin', let him finish it."

"Go ahead, Sackett," Shore said. "I want to hear this."

"Larnie Cagle slipped away from night-herding and rode over to the Fetchen camp. He told them all they wanted to know. He told them about Galloway, Moss, and me, and if we hadn't made it sooner than expected, we'd have been trapped and killed. They'd have followed with an attack on this camp."

Cagle was watching me, expecting me to draw, but he was stalling, waiting for the edge.

"Nobody is going to believe that," he said, almost carelessly.

"They will believe it," Judith said suddenly. It was the first thing she had said since coming into camp. "Because I saw you, too. And that wasn't the first time. He had been there before."

Suddenly all the smartness had gone out of him. Cagle stood there like a trapped animal. He had not seen Judith, and had no idea she was in camp.

"What about it, Cagle?" Hawkes's tone was cold.

"Mr. Hawkes," Kyle Shore said, "this here is my deal. I rode into camp with him, we hired on together."

He turned to Cagle. "Larnie, when I ride, I ride for the brand. I may sell my gun, but it stays sold."

Briggs rode up to the edge of the firelight. "They're comin', Mr. Hawkes. They're all around us."

"You ain't got a chance!" Cagle said with a sneer in his voice. "You never had a chance."

"You've got one," Kyle Shore said. "You've got just one, Larnie, but you got to kill me to get it."

They looked at each other across the fire, and Shore said, "I never rode with no double-crosser, and never will. I figure you're my fault."

Cagle gave a laugh, but the laugh was a little shrill. "You? Why, you damn' fool, you never saw the day you —"

He dropped his hand, and he was fast. His gun cleared the holster and came up shooting.

The first shot hit the dirt at Shore's feet and the second shot cut a notch from his hat brim.

Kyle Shore had drawn almost as fast, but his gun came up smoothly, and taking his time he shot . . . just once.

Larnie Cagle took a teetering step forward, then fell on his face, dead before he touched the ground.

"Damn' fool," Shore said. "He surely fancied that fast draw. I told him he should take time. Make the first shot count. He wouldn't listen."

Out upon the plains there was a shot, then another. We ran for our horses, bunching them under the trees. Galloway dropped to one knee near a tree trunk and fired quickly at a racing horse, then again. Taking Judith by the hand, I pushed her down behind a big fallen tree. Then I knelt beside her, rifle up, hunting a target.

There was a flurry of hammering shots and then the pound of racing hoofs, and they were gone. When Black saw there was no surprise, he just lit up the night with a little rifle fire and rode off, figuring there'd be another day . . . as there generally is.

Daylight took its time a-coming, and some of us waited by the fire nursing our coffee cups in chilly fingers, our shoulders hunched. Others dozed against a fallen log, and a few crawled back into their blankets and catnapped the last two hours away.

Me, I moved restlessly around camp, picking up fuel for the fire, contemplating what we'd best do next. Evan Hawkes would be wanting to get the rest of his cattle back; but now that we had Judith again, it was our duty to carry her west to her pa.

There was a sight of work to do, and some of the cattle would be scratched or battered from horns or brush, and unless they were cared for we'd have blowflies settling on them. A cowhand's work is never done. He ropes and rides before sunup and rarely gets in for chow before the sun is down.

Judith, she slept — slept like a baby. But she worried me some, looking at her. She didn't look much like a little girl any more, and looking at a girl thataway can confuse a man's thinking.

My fingers touched my jaw. It had been some time since I'd shaved, and I'd best be about it before we got to riding westward again.

Kyle Shore wasn't talking. He was sitting there looking into the fire, his back to the long bundle we'd bury, come daybreak. I had Shore pegged now. He was a good, steady man, a fighter by trade, with no pretense to being a real gunman. He was no fast-draw artist, but his kind could kill a lot who thought they were.

Thinking about that, I went for coffee. It was hot, blacker than sin, and strong enough to float a horseshoe. It was cowboy's coffee.

Chapter 8

Morning, noon, and night we worked our hearts out, rounding up the scattered herd, and when we had finished we still lacked a lot of having half of what Evan Hawkes had started with when he left Texas. The Fetchen outfit had made off with the rest of them.

After a week of riding and rounding them up we started west once more.

Judith was quiet. She pulled her weight around camp, helping the cook and generally making herself useful, and when she was on the range she showed that she not only could ride the rough string but that she could savvy cattle.

Much as I wanted to pay her no mind, it was getting so I couldn't do that. She was around camp, stirring pots, bending over the fire, and looking so pretty I wondered whether I'd been right in the head when I first put eyes on her back yonder in Tazewell.

Nonetheless, I kept my eyes off her as much as I could. I rode out from camp early, and avoided sitting nigh her when it was possible. Only it seemed we were always winding up sitting side by side. I never talked or said much. First off, I'm simply no hand with women. Galloway now, he had half the girls in the mountains breathing hard most of the time, but me, I was just big and quiet, and when I was seated by womenfolks all the words in me just lost themselves in the breaks of my mind. No matter how much I tried, I couldn't put a loop over even one sentence.

Besides, there was the land. A big, grand, wide country with every glance lost in the distance. There was a special feeling on the wind when it blew across those miles of grass, a wind so cool, so deep down inside you that every breath of it was like a drink of cool water. And we saw the tumbleweeds far out ahead of us, hundreds of them rolling south ahead of the wind, like the skirmish line of an army.

At first they made the cattle skittish, but they got used to them, as we did. I never knew where they came from, but for three days the wind blew cool out of the north and for three days they came in the hundreds, in the thousands.

Trees grew thicker along the streams, and the grass was better. From time to time we saw scattered buffalo, three or four together, and once a big old bull, alone on a hilltop, watching us pass. He followed us for two days, keeping his distance — wanting company I suppose.

Twice we saw burned-out wagons, places where Indians had rounded up some settlers. Nobody would ever know who they were, and folks back home would wonder about them for a while, and then time would make them become dimmer.

Like Galloway and me. We had no close kinfolk, nobody keeping account of us. If we were to get killed out here nobody would ask who, why, or whatever. It made a body feel kind of lonesome down inside, and it set me to wondering where I was headed for.

Once, far ahead of the herd, I heard a galloping behind me, and when I turned in the saddle I saw it was that Judith girl. She rode side-saddle, of course, and looked mighty fetching as she came up to me.

"You'd be a sight better off with the rest," I said. "If we met up with Indians, you might get taken."

"I'm not afraid. Not with you to care for me."

Now, that there remark just about threw me. I suppose nobody had ever said such a thing to me before, and it runs in the blood of a man that he should care for womenfolk. It's a need in him, deep as motherhood to a woman, and it's a thing folks are likely to forget. A man with nobody to care for is as lonesome as a lost hound dog, and as useless. If he's to feel of any purpose to himself, he's got to feel he's needed, feel he stands between somebody and any trouble.

I'd had nobody. Galloway was fit to care for himself and an army of others. He was a man built for action, and tempered to violence. Gentle, he was most times, but fierce when aroused. You might as well try to take care of a grizzly bear as of him. So I'd had nobody, nor had he.

"I'd stand up for you," I said, "but it would be a worrisome thing to have to think of somebody else. I mean, whilst fighting, or whatever. Anyway, you'd take off after that Fetchen outfit if they showed up."

"I would not!"

She put her chin up at me, but stayed alongside, and said nothing more for a while.

"Mighty pretty country," I ventured after a bit.

"It is, isn't it? I just can't wait to see Pa's ranch." She sobered down then. "I hope he's all right."

"You worried about the Fetchens?"

"Yes, I am. You've no idea what they are like.

I just never imagined men could be like that." She looked quickly at me. "Oh, they were all right to me. James saw to that. But I heard talk when they didn't think I was listening." She turned toward me again. "The happiest moment in my life was when you came from behind that tree trunk. And you might have been killed!"

"Yes, ma'am. That's a common might-have-been out here. There's few things a man can do that might not get him killed. It's a rough land, but a man is better off if he rides his trail knowing there may be trouble about. It simply won't do to get careless. . . . And you be careful, too."

A pretty little stream, not over eight or ten inches deep, but running at a lively pace, and kind of curving around a flat meadow with low hills offered shelter from the north, and a cluster of cottonwoods and willows where we could camp . . . it was just what we needed.

"We'll just sort of camp here," I said. "I'll ride over and get a cooking fire started."

"Flagan!" Judith screamed, and I wheeled and saw three of them come up out of the grass near that stream where they'd been laying for me.

Three of them rising right up out of the ground, like, with their horses nowhere near them, and all three had their rifles on me.

Instinctively, I swung my horse. He was a good cutting horse who could turn on a dime and have six cents left, and he turned now. When he wheeled about I charged right at them. My six-shooter was in my hand, I don't know how come, and I chopped down with it, blasting a shot at the nearest one while keeping him between the others and me.

Swinging my horse again, I doubled right back on my heels in charging down on the others. I heard a bullet nip by me, felt a jolt somewhere, and then I was firing again and the last man was legging it for the cottonwoods. I taken in after him as he ran, and I came up alongside him and nudged him with the horse to knock him rolling.

I turned my horse again and came back on him as he was staggering to his feet. I let the horse come alongside him again, and this time I lifted a stirrup and caught him right in the middle with my heel. It knocked him all sprawled out.

One of the others was getting up and was halfway to his horse by the time I could get around to him, but I started after him too. He made it almost to the brush before I gave him my heel, knocking him face down into the broken branches of the willows.

Judith had now ridden up to me. "Are you hurt?" she asked.

"Not me. Those boys are some upset, I figure." I looked at her. "You warned me," I said. "You yelled just in time."

Three riders had come over the hill, riding hell bent for election. They were Galloway, Kyle Shore, and Hawkes himself, all of them with rifles ready for whatever trouble there was.

There was only blood on the grass where the first man had fallen. He had slipped off into the tall grass and brush, and had no doubt got to his horse and away. One of the others was also gone, but he was hurting — I'd lay a bit of money on that. The last man I'd kicked into the brush looked as if he'd been fighting a couple of porcupines. His face was a sight, scratched and bloody like nothing a body ever saw.

"You near broke my back!" he complained. "What sort of way is that to do a man up?"

"You'd rather get shot?"

He looked at me. "I reckon not," he said dryly, "if given the choice."

"You're a Burshill by the look of you," I said.

"I'm Trent Burshill, cousin to the Fetchens."

"You might be in better comp'ny. But I know your outfit. You folks have been making 'shine back in the hills since before Noah."

"Nigh to a hunert years," he said proudly.

"No Burshill of my line never paid no tax on whiskey."

"You should have stayed back there. You aren't going to cut the mustard in these western lands. Now you've mixed up in rustling."

"You got it to prove."

Kyle Shore looked hard at him. "Friend, you'd best learn. Out here they hold court in the saddle and execute the sentence with a saddle rope."

"You fixin' to hang me?"

"Dunno," Shore said, straight-faced. "It depends on Mr. Hawkes. If he sees fit to hang you, that's what we'll do."

Trent Burshill looked pretty unhappy. "I never counted on that," he said. "Seemed like this was wide-open land where a man could do as he liked."

"As long as you don't interfere with no other man," Shore said. "Western folks look down on that. And they've got no time to be ridin' to court, maybe a hundred miles, just to hang a cow thief. A cottonwood limb works better."

Trent Burshill looked thoughtful. "Should be a way of settling this," he said. "Sure, I lined up with Black, him being my cousin an' all."

"Where's Black headed for?" I asked.

He glanced around at me. "You're one of them Tennessee Sacketts. I heard tell of you.

124

Why, he's headed for the Greenhorns — some mountains westward. He's got him some idea about them."

Burshill looked at me straight. "He aims to do you in, Sackett. Was I you, I'd be travelin' east, not west."

The rest of the outfit were trailing into the bottom now with the herd. I spotted a thick limb overhead. "There's a proper branch," I said. "Maybe we ought to tie his hands, put the noose over his neck, and leave him in the saddle. Give him a chance to see how long his horse would stand without moving."

Trent Burshill looked up at the limb over his head. "If you boys was to reconsider," he said, "I'd like to ride for Tennessee. These last few minutes," he added, "Tennessee never looked so good."

"That puncher with the scar on his face," I said to him, "that newcomer. Now, who would he be?"

Burshill shrugged. "You can have him. I figure he deserves the rope more than me. Personal, I don't cotton to him. He's snake-mean. That there is Russ Menard."

Kyle Shore looked at me. "Sackett, you've bought yourself trouble. Russ Menard is reckoned by some to be the fastest man with a gun and the most dangerous anywhere about."

"I knew a man like that once," I said.

"Where is he?"

"Why, he's dead. He proved to be not so fast as another man, and not so dangerous with three bullets in him."

"Russ Menard," Shore said, "comes from down in the Nation. He killed one of Judge Parker's marshals and figured it was healthier out of his jurisdiction. He was in a gun battle in Tascosa, and some say he was in the big fight in Lincoln, New Mexico."

Evan Hawkes, who had ridden over to locate his chuck wagon and crew, now came back. Judith Costello rode beside him. Harry Briggs and Ladder Walker drifted along, leading a horse.

"Found his horse," Hawkes said.

"Tie him on it," Walker said, "backwards in the saddle, and turn him loose."

"Now, see here!" Burshill protested.

"Then take his boots off and let him walk back. I heard about a man walked a hundred miles once, in his bare feet!"

"Way I heard it," Burshill said, "was there would be land and cattle and horses for the taking. A man could get rich, that's what Black said. I never figured on no rope."

"The land's for the taking," Hawkes said, "but the cattle and the horses belong to somebody.

126

You have helped in rustling, and you were about to dry-gulch my men. What have you to say for yourself?"

"I made good whiskey. It was 'shine, but it was good whiskey," Burshill said. "I wouldn't want to grieve my kinfolk back in Tennessee."

"I'll let you have your horse," Evan Hawkes said, "but if we see you west of here we'll hang you."

"Mister, you let me go now, and you'll have to burn the stump and sift the ashes before you find me again."

"All right, Hawkes said, "let him go."

Trent Burshill lit out of there as if his tail was afire, and that was just as well. I wasn't strong on hanging, anyway.

When the night fire was burning and there was the smell of coffee in the air, I went to Evan Hawkes.

"Mr. Hawkes, Galloway and me, we figure we'd best light out of here and head for Costello's ranch in the Greenhorns. If the Fetchens come on him unprepared they might ride him down. We can make faster time free of the herd."

"All right. I'm sorry to lose you boys, but we're heading the same way." He paused. "I'm going to get my herd back, so you boys figure yourselves still on the payroll. When you get that girl back to her father, you roust around and locate my cattle for me."

By daylight we had the camp well behind us. The horses we rode were good, fast ones with a lot of stamina. Judith was a rider, all right, and we stayed with it all day, riding the sun out of the sky, and soon we could see the far-off jagged line of mountains. The stars came up.

We slept in a tiny hollow under some cotton-woods, the horses grazing, and the remains of a small fire smoking under the coffeepot. Me, I was first up as always, putting sticks and bark together with a twist of dried grass to get the flame going, but keeping my ears alert for sound. At times I prowled to the edge of the hollow and looked around.

Back at camp Galloway still slept, wrapped in his blanket, but Judith lay with her cheek pillowed on her arm, her dark hair around her face, her lips soft in the morning light. It made a man restless to see her so, and I turned back to my fire.

Judith Costello . . . it was a lovely name. But even if I was of a mind to, what could I offer such a girl? Her family were movers, they were horse-traders and traveling folks, but from all I'd heard they were well-off. And me, I had a gun and a saddle.

My thoughts turned to the ranch in the Greenhorns. The Fetchens had killed Judith's grandpa back in Tennessee, more than likely in anger at Judith and because of the loss of the horses. But suppose there was something more? Suppose the Fetchen outfit knew something we did not even surmise?

First of all, it was needful for us to ride west to that ranch, and not come on it unexpected, either. It was in my mind to circle about, to look the place over before riding right in. I had no idea what sort of a man Costello was, or how much of an outfit he had, but it would do no harm to sort of prospect around before making ourselves known.

We put together a breakfast from provisions we'd brought from Hawkes's outfit, then saddled up and rode west, keeping always to low ground.

The Greenhorns were a small range, a sort of offshoot of the towering Sangre de Cristos. It was Ute country, and although the Utes were said to be quiet, I wasn't any too sure of it, and I was taking no chances.

First off, we had to locate Costello's ranch, for all we had in the way of directions was that it was in the Greenhorns. The nearest town I knew of was Walsenburg, but I wanted to avoid towns. Sure as shootin', the Fetchens would have somebody around to let them know of us coming. North of there, and about due west of us, was a stage stop called Greenhorn, and at the Greenhorn Inn, one of Kit Carson's old hangouts, we figured it was likely we'd hear something.

Big a country as it was, most everybody knew of all the ranchers and settlers around, and the place was small enough so we could see about everything in it before we rode into town — if town it could be called.

We made our nooning on the Huerfano River about ten miles east of Greenhorn, and made a resting time of it, for I wanted to ride into the place about sundown.

Galloway was restless, and I knew just what he felt. There was that much between us that we each knew the other's feelings. He could sense trouble coming, and was on edge for it. We both knew it was there, not far off, and waiting for us like a set trap.

There was a good deal of hate in the Fetchens, and it was in Black most of all; and they would not rest until they'd staked our hides out to dry, or we had come it over them the final time.

When noon was well past, we mounted up and pushed on to Greenhorn. The mountains were named for an Indian chief who had ruled the roost around there in times gone by. It was said of the young buck deer when his horns were fresh and in velvet that he was a "green-horn," for he was foolishly brave then, ready to challenge anything. The chief had been that way, too, but the Spanish wiped him out. So the name greenhorn was given to anyone young and braver than he had right to be, going in where angels fear to tread, as the saying is.

The Greenhorn Inn was a comfortable enough place, as such places went — a stage stop and a hotel with sleeping quarters and a fair-to-middling dining room. We rode up, tied our horses out of sight, and the three of us checked the horses in the stable, but we saw none we recognized as Fetchen horses.

The place was nigh to empty. One old codger with a face that looked as if it was carved out of flint was sitting there, and he looked at us as if he'd seen us before, although I knew no such face. He was a lean, savage-looking old man, one of those old buffalo hunters or mountain men, by the look of him — nobody to have much truck with.

The man behind the bar glanced at Judith and then at us. We found a table and hung our hats nearby, then sat down. He came over to us.

"How are you, folks? We've got beans and bacon, beans and bear meat, beans and venison. You name it. And we've got fresh-baked bread . . . made it my ownself."

We ordered, and he brought us coffee, black and strong. Tasting it, I glanced over at Judith. For a girl facing up to trouble, she looked bright and pretty, just too pretty for a mountain boy like me.

"This here," I said to her, "is right touchy country. There's Indians about, both Utes and Comanches, and no matter what anybody says there's angry blood in them. They don't like white men very much, and they don't like each other."

"I can't think of anything but Pa," she said. "It has been such a long time since I've seen him, and now that we are so close, I can hardly sit still for wanting to be riding on."

"You hold your horses," Galloway advised. "We'll make it in time."

Even as he spoke, I had an odd feeling of foreboding come over me. It was such a feeling as I'd never had before. I looked across at Galloway, and he was looking at me, and we both knew what the other felt.

What was going to happen? What was lying in wait for us?

When the man came back with our food I looked up at him and said, "We're hunting the Costello outfit, over in the Greenhorns. Can you tell us how to get there?"

He put the dishes down in front of us before

we got an answer. "My advice to you is to stay away from there. It will get you nothing but trouble."

Judith's face went pale under the tan, and her eyes were suddenly frightened.

When I spoke, my voice was rougher than I intended, because of her. "What do you mean by that?"

The man backed off a step, in no way intimidated, simply wary. "I mean that's a tough outfit over there. You go in there hunting trouble and you're likely to find it."

"We aren't seeking it out," I said, more quietly. "Costello is this lady's pa. We're taking her home."

"Sorry, ma'am," he said quietly. "I didn't know. If I were you, I'd ride careful. There's been trouble in those hills."

It was not until we had finished eating that he spoke to us again. "You boys drop around later," he said, "and I'll buy you a drink."

At the door, hesitating before going to her room, Judith looked from Galloway to me. "He's going to tell you something, isn't he? I mean that's why he offered to buy you a drink, to get you back there without me."

"Now, I don't think —" Galloway interrupted.

She would have none of it. "Flagan, you'll tell me, won't you? I've got to know if there's anything wrong. I've simply got to! After all, I haven't seen Pa in a long time."

"I'll tell you," I said, though I knew I might be lying in my teeth, for I figured she'd guessed right. That man had something to relate, and it was likely something he didn't want Judith to hear.

She turned and went to her room, and we stayed a minute, Galloway and me, hesitating to go back.

Chapter 9

We stood there together, having it in our heads that what we would hear would bring us no pleasure. The night was closing in around us, and no telling what would come to Greenhorn whilst we were abed. Whatever it was, we could expect nothing but grief.

"Before we go to bed," Galloway suggested, "we'd better take a turn around outside."

"You sleep under cover," I said. "I'll make out where I can listen well. I'd not sleep easy otherwise."

"I ain't slept in a bed for some time," Galloway said, "but I'm pining to."

"You have at it. I'll find a place where my ears can pick up sound whilst I sleep."

We walked back into the saloon, two mountain boys from Tennessee. The old man still sat at his table, staying long over his coffee. He shot a hard glance at us, but we trailed on up to the bar.

The bartender poured each of us a drink, then gestured toward a table. "We might as well sit down. There'll be nobody else along tonight, and there's no sense in standing when you can sit."

"That's a fine-looking young lady," he said after we were seated. "I'd want no harm to come to her, but there's talk of trouble over there, and Costello is right in the midst of it."

We waited, and there was no sound in the room. Finally he spoke again, his face oddly lighted by the light from the coal-oil lamp with the reflector behind it. "There's something wrong up there — I don't know what it is. Costello used to come down here once in a while . . . the last time was a year ago. I was over that way, but he wouldn't see me. Ordered me off the place."

"Why?"

"Well, it was his place. I suppose he had his reasons." The bartender refilled the glasses from the bottle. "Nevertheless it worried me, because it wasn't like him. . . . He lives alone, you know, back over on the ridge.'"

He paused again, then went on, "He fired his hands, all of them."

"He's alone up there now?"

"I don't think so. A few days back there were

some men came riding up here, asked where Costello's layout was."

"Like we did," I said.

"I told them. I had no reason not to, although I didn't like their looks, but I also warned them they wouldn't be welcome. They laughed at me. One of them spoke up and said that they'd be welcome, all right, that Costello was expecting them."

"They beat us to it, Flagan," Galloway said. "They're here."

The bartender glanced from one to the other of us. "You know those men?"

"We know them, and if any of them show up again, be careful. They'll kill you as soon as look at you . . . maybe sooner."

"What are you two going to do?"

"Go up there. We gave a fair promise to see the young lady to her pa. So we'll go up there."

"And those men?"

Galloway grinned at him, then at me. "Why, they'd better light a shuck for Texas before we tie cans to their tails."

"Those men, now," I said, "did they have any cattle?"

"Not with them. But they said they had a herd following." He paused. "Is there anything I can do? There's good folks in this country, and Costello was a good neighbor, although a man

137

who kept to himself except when needed. If it comes to that, we could round up a goodly lot who would ride to help him."

"You leave it to us. We Sacketts favor skinning our own cats."

The old man seated alone at the table spoke up then. "I knowed it. I knowed you two was Sacketts. I'm Cap Rountree, an' I was with Tyrel and them down on the Mogollon that time."

"Heard you spoken of," Galloway said. "Come on over and set."

"If you boys are ridin' into trouble," Rountree said, "I'd admire to ride along. I been sharin' Sackett trouble a good few years now, and I don't feel comfortable without it."

We talked a spell, watching the night hours pass, and listening for the sounds of riders who did not come.

Black Fetchen must have sent riders on ahead, and those riders must have moved in fast and hard. He might even have gone on ahead himself, letting the herd follow. We would have ridden right into a trap had we just gone on ahead without making inquiries, or being a mite suspicious.

"Hope he's all right," I said. "Costello, I mean. It would go hard with Judith to lose her pa as well as her grandpa all to once, like that."

"Well, I'll see you boys, come daylight," Rountree said. "I'm holed up in the stable should you need me."

"I'll be around off and on all night," I told him. "Don't shoot until you see the whites of my eyes."

Cap walked outside, stood there a moment, and then went off into the darkness.

"I like that old man," Galloway said. "Seems to me Tyrel set store by him."

"One of his oldest friends. Came west with him from eastern Kansas, where they tied up on a trail herd."

"We'll need him," Galloway added. "We're facing up to trouble, Flagan."

"You get some sleep," I advised. "I'll do the same."

Outside it was still. Off to the west I thought I could see the gleam of snow on the mountains. I liked the smell of the wind off those peaks, but after a minute I walked tiredly across the road, picked up my blanket and poncho, and bedded down under a cottonwood where I could hear the trail sounds in the night. If any riders came up to the Greenhorn Inn I wanted to be the first to know.

Tired as I was, I didn't sleep, my thoughts wandering, just thinking of Galloway and me, homeless as tumbleweeds, drifting loose around the country. It was time we found land, time we put down some roots. It did a man no good to ride about always feathered for trouble. Sooner or later he would wind up dead, back in some draw or on some windy slope, leaving his carcass for the coyotes and buzzards to fight over. It doesn't matter how tough a man becomes, or how good he is with a gun, there comes the time when his draw is a little too slow, or something gets in the way of his bullet.

We were rougher than cobs, Galloway and me, but in this country many a tough man had cashed in his chips. It wasn't in me to think lightly of Black Fetchen. He was known throughout the mountains for his fist fighting and shooting, a man of terrible rages and fierce hatreds . . . we weren't going to come it over him without grief.

Suddenly, I came wide awake. I had no idea just when I'd dozed off, but my eyes came wide open and I was listening. What I heard was a horse walking . . . two horses.

My hand closed on my gun butt.

There was no light showing anywhere in any of the four or five buildings that made up Greenhorn. The inn was dark and still.

The first thing I made out was the shine of a horse's hip, then the glisten of starlight on a rifle barrel. Two riders had pulled up in the road right in front of the inn. A saddle creaked . . . one man was getting down.

Our horses were out back, picketed on a stretch of meadow. Unless those riders scouted around some they'd not be likely to find them, for the meadow was back beyond the corral and stable.

Noiselessly I sat up, keeping the blanket hunched around my shoulders, for the night was chill. I held my .45 in my hand, the barrel across my thigh.

After a bit I heard boots crunching and the rider came back. By now I could almost make him out — a big man with a kind of rolling walk. "Ain't there," I heard him whisper. "At least, their horses aren't in the stalls or the corral."

He stepped into the saddle again and I listened as they walked their horses down the road. Beyond the buildings they stepped them up to a trot, and I wondered where they figured to lay up for the night. It seemed to me they might have a place in mind. Come daylight, if they didn't find our tracks on the trail, they might just hole up and wait for us.

I dozed off, and when next I awakened the sky was getting bright. I rolled my bed and led the horses in, gave them an easy bait of water, and had all three horses saddled before Galloway came out of the inn.

"They're a-fixing to eat in there," he said. "It smells almighty nice."

Cap Rountree came from the stable, leading a raw-boned roan gelding, under a worn-out saddle packing two rifle scabbards. He glanced at me and I grinned at him.

"I take it your visitor wasn't talking much," I said.

"Didn't see me," Cap said, "an' just as well. I had my old Bowie to hand, and had he offered trouble I'd have split his brisket. I don't take to folks prowlin' about in the dark."

"Fetchen men?" Galloway asked.

"I reckon. Leastways, they were hunting somebody. They went on up the road."

Rountree tied his horse alongside ours. "You boys new to this country? I rode through here in the fall of 1830, my first time. And a time or two after that." He nodded toward the mountains. "I brought a load of fur out of those mountains two jumps ahead of a pack o' Utes.

"Ran into Bridger and some of his outfit, holed in behind a stream bank. I made it to them, and those Utes never knew what hit 'em. They'd no idea there was another white man in miles, nor did I. . . . Good fighters, them Utes."

He started across the street toward the inn.

"Point is," he stopped to say, "I can take you right up to Costello's outfit without usin' no trail."

Judith was waiting for us, looking pretty as a bay pony with three white stockings. We all sat up, and the bartender, innkeeper, or whatever, brought on the eggs and bacon. We put away six eggs apiece and most of a side of bacon, it seemed like. At least, Galloway and me ate that many eggs. Judith was content with three, and Cap about the same.

An hour later we were up in the pines, hearing the wind rushing through them like the sound of the sea on a beach. Cap Rountree led the way, following no trail that a body could see, yet he rode sure and true, up and through mountains that reminded us of home.

Presently Cap turned in his saddle. "These Fetchens, now. You said they rustled the Hawkes herd. You ever hear talk of them hunting gold?"

"We had no converse with them," Galloway said, "but I know there was some talk of a Fetchen going to the western mountains many years back."

"Fetchen?" Cap Rountree puzzled over the name. "I figured I knowed most of the old-timers, but I recall no Fetchen. Reason I mentioned it, this here country is full of lost mines.

The way folks tell it, there's lost mines or caches of gold all over this country."

He pointed toward the west and south. "There lie the Spanish Peaks, with many a legend about them of sun gods an' rain gods, and of gold, hidden or found.

"North of here there's a cave in Marble Mountain, called the Caverna del Oro, where there's supposed to be gold. I never did hear of gold in a natural cave unless it was cached there, but that's possible. Those old Spanish men rode all over this country.

"There's a man named Sharp lives over there yonder," he went on. "Got him a place called Buzzard Roost Ranch and he's made friends with the Utes. He probably knows more about those old mines than anybody, although I don't rec'lect him wastin' time a-huntin' for them."

Half a mile further he drew up to let the horses take a blow. "I was thinkin' that maybe the Fetchen outfit knew something you boys don't," he said. He threw a sharp glance at Judith. "You ever hear your grandpa talk of any gold mines or such?" he asked her.

Then he said to us, "You told me the Fetchens murdered him. D' you suppose they wanted something besides this here girl? Or the horses?"

He grinned slyly at Judith. "Meanin' no offense, ma'am, for was I a younger man I might do murder myself for such a pretty girl."

"That's all right," Judith said. "I'm used to it." After a moment, she shook her head. "No, there's nothing that I can recall."

"Now, think of this a mite. Yours is a horse-tradin' family, and they stick together. I know about the Irish traders — I spent time in country where they traded. Seems unusual one of them would cut off from the rest like your pa done. D' you suppose he knew something? Maybe when he got to swappin' around, he took something in trade he didn't talk about."

The more I considered what Cap was saying the more I wondered if he hadn't made a good guess. That Fetchen outfit were a murdering lot by all accounts, but why should they kill Costello? What could they hope to gain?

It was possible, trading around like they had done, that one of the Costellos might have picked up a map or a treasure story in trade. Maybe thrown in as boot by somebody who did not believe it themselves.

Now there was a new idea that would account for a lot.

"You consider it," I said to Judith. "Come morning, you may recall something said or seen."

There were a lot of folks scattered through the East who had gone west and then returned to the States – some to get married, some because they liked the easier life, some because they figured the risk of getting their hair lifted by a Comanche was too great. It might be that one of them had known something; or maybe some western man, dying, had sent a map to some of his kinfolk.

We had been following Rountree up an old Indian trail through the high country, but now we saw a valley before us, still some distance off. He drew up again and pointed ahead.

"Right down there is Sharp's trading post, the Buzzard Roost. Closer to us, but out of sight, is the town of Badito.

"Some of the finest horseflesh you ever did see, right down in that valley," he added.

"Costello's?"

"His an' Sharp's. Tom Sharp went back to Missouri in seventy-one and bought himself about thirty, forty, head o' stock, a thoroughbred racer among them. Then he sent north into Idaho and bought about two hundred head of appaloosa's from the Nez Percé. He's bred them together for some tough, hardy stock."

"That's what Pa and Grandpa were doing," Judith said.

Well, I looked over at her. "Judith, was your

146

pa in Missouri in seventy-one? I mean, it might have been him or some of his kinfolk who made a deal with Sharp. The tie-up might be right there."

"I don't know," she said doubtfully. "I was just a little girl. We were in Missouri in that year or the next, I think, but I never paid much attention . . . we were always moving."

We camped in the woods that night, smelling the pines, and eating venison we'd killed ourselves. It was a good night, and we sat late around the fire, just talking and yarning of this and that. Galloway and me, we sang a mite, for all we mountain boys take to singing, especially those of Welsh extraction like us.

It was a fine, beautiful night, and one I'd not soon forget, and for once we felt safe. Not that one or the other of us didn't get up once in a while and move away from the fire to prowl around and listen.

Tomorrow we were heading down into the valley, for we had decided to talk to Tom Sharp. Cap knew him, and he had been a friend to Costello. If there was anything to be found out, we would learn it from him.

But I was uneasy. I'd got to thinking about that girl too much, and it worried me. When a man gets mixed up in a shooting affair he'd best keep his mind about him, and not be contemplating a girl's face and a pair of lovely lips.

When we tangled with the Fetchens again they would be out for blood. They had got where they were going, but we had won several hands from them . . . now they would try to make us pay for it. We were few, and there was nowhere about that we could look for help.

Cap gestured off toward the western mountains. "Just over there Tell Sackett an' me had quite a shindig a while back. Believe me, they know the name of Sackett in that country."

I knew about Tell. I'd heard all that talk down in the Mogollon. The trouble was, mostly we Sacketts were noted for our fighting ways, except maybe for Tyrel, who had become a rancher, and Orrin, who was in politics. It was time some of us did something worthwhile, time we made a mark in the country for something besides gunplay.

A man who rides a violent road comes to only one end – up a dry creek somewhere, or on Boot Hill.

Chapter 10

Tom Sharp was a fine-looking man, the kind you'd ride the river with. He was pushing forty. He had been wounded in the War Between the States, had come west, hunted meat for the mining camps, and cut telegraph poles on contract for the Union Pacific. Finally he'd traveled up the old Ute trail to Huerfano River and opened a trading post in the valley in a big adobe building.

Right off, he started to improve both his horses and cattle by bringing in blooded stock from the States. He was not one of those who came west to get rich and get out; he came to stay and to build. The town of Malachite grew up around his trading post.

As we came riding up to the trading post, he came outside and stood on the steps to meet us, giving us a careful study. All I needed was one glimpse of Sharp to know that he

149

was a man who would stand for no nonsense, and he certainly would not cotton to the likes of Black Fetchen.

"Mr. Sharp?" I said. "I'm Flagan Sackett, this here is my brother Galloway, and our friend Cap Rountree. The young lady is Judith Costello."

Now, mayhap that wasn't just the way to introduce folks, but I wanted Tom Sharp to know who we were right off, for if a lot of tough strangers had been coming into the country, he would not be in a trusting mood.

He ignored me, looking first at Judith, for which I didn't blame him. "How are you, Judith? Your father has spoken of you."

"Is he all right? I mean . . . we haven't heard, and those men . . ."

"He was all right the last I saw of him, but that's been over a month ago. Will you get down and come in? The wife will be wanting to talk to you, and I'm sure you could all do with some food."

Whilst the rest of them went in, I led the horses to water. After a bit Tom Sharp came out, and gave a look at the horses. "Fine stock," he said. "Is that some of the Costello brand?"

"Yes, it is. We've taken the responsibility of bringing Judith out here to her pa, but there's been trouble along the way. With the Fetchens."

"I have heard of them," Sharp said grimly, "and nothing good. And it isn't the first time."

I gave him a surprised glance. "You've run into them before? You surely ain't from Tennessee?"

"From Missouri. No, it wasn't back there. A few years ago we had a sight of trouble over east and north of here with the Reynolds gang, and one of the gang was a Fetchen. They were some connection of the Reynolds outfit, I never did know what it was. The Reynolds outfit were wiped out, but Fetchen wasn't among those killed."

"Which one was he?"

"Tirey Fetchen. He'd be about my age now. He was a wanted man even before he tied up with the Reynolds gang. I'd had wanted circulars on him when I was a deputy sheriff up in Wyoming, maybe twelve years back, and I recall they listed killings back before the war. He was with the Reynolds gang during the war."

We stabled the horses, and then I went inside. The rest of them were gathered around a table eating, and that food surely smelled good.

"We've seen them come in," Sharp told us over coffee, "but not to stay around. They'd show up, then head for the hills." He looked around at me. "If they've gone up to Costello's place, he may be in real trouble."

151

"If Judith can stay here," I suggested, "we'll ride up and look around."

"I'll not stay!" Judith exclaimed.

"Now, ma'am," Sharp protested.

"I mean it. I have come all the way to see my father, and I won't wait any longer. I'm going with you." Then she added, looking right at me, "If you don't take me I'll go by myself."

Well, I looked over at Galloway and he shrugged, and that was all there was to it. Both of us knew there was no time to be gained arguing with a woman, and we'd both had a try before this at arguing with Judith.

She went off with Mrs. Sharp, and Sharp sat down with us. "You boys better ride careful," he said. "That's a bad outfit."

So we told him about the trip west and the loss of the Hawkes herd, the Half-Box H.

Sharp was thoughtful. When he looked up at us he said, "I'd better warn you, and when Hawkes comes along you'd better warn him. Fetchen registered a brand in his own name, the JBF Connected."

Cap chuckled. "Ain't takin' him a while to learn. A JBF Connected would fit right over a Half-Box H, fit it like a glove. If Hawkes ain't right careful he'll find all his herd wearin' the wrong brand."

I looked at Sharp. "How are folks hereabouts?

Are they understandin'?"

"That depends."

"Maybe the only way we can get those cattle back is to rustle them," I said. "If he can misbrand cattle, we can just brand 'em over."

"What about that?" Galloway said. "What would cover a JBF Connected?"

"When we were ridin' through Texas," I suggested, "we saw a man down there who had a Pig-Pen brand. And I heard tell of one with a Spider-Web. They would cover most anything you could dream up."

"You would have to be careful," Sharp said. "And if you will forgive me, I would have to see Hawkes's papers on the herd."

"He's got 'em, and he'll be showing up right quick." I paused a minute, giving it thought. "What we figured, would be to sort of let the word get around. I mean, about Hawkes's herd and what he figures to do about it."

Sharp chuckled. "Now, that could be right amusing. But you'd have to move fast. It is about roundup time."

"So much the better. A lot of things can happen during a roundup. Only thing we want is to have it understood this is strictly between us and the Fetchen crowd."

"Serve them right," Sharp said. "You just wait until word gets around. You'll have the

153

whole country on your side."

Nevertheless, I was worried. We had to get back into the hills and scout around the Costello outfit, and we had to see Costello himself, but Galloway and me, we knew that every step of the way would be a step further into trouble. Whatever the Fetchens were up to, they were also laying a trap for us, and we were riding up there, maybe right into the trap.

The more we learned, the more we had to worry about. Evan Hawkes was still far behind us, whilst the Fetchens were here, and in considerable strength. Along the line they had picked up more men, outlaws and the like.

But what was it that Black Fetchen was really after? What lay behind their move west? Had it been simply because of their killing of Laban Costello? And for revenge on us? Or was there some deeper cause that began even before we showed up? Was it something they wanted even more than Judith, more than the horses, more than Costello's ranch, if that was what they aimed for?

The thing that stuck in my mind was that Tirey Fetchen had stirred about in these parts before any of us came west, and with the Reynolds gang. Now, there was something about that . . . I couldn't recall what it was, but something I'd heard about that Reynolds outfit.

They had been a gang of outlaws who passed it off that they were robbing to get money for the Confederacy, or that was the tale I'd heard. They had been caught up with, and some of them had been tied to a tree and shot. I had nothing to say about that part of it to anybody, because I wanted to recall what it was about the Reynolds gang that made me remember them . . . some item I'd forgotten.

We went into the hills, climbing high up by an old Ute trail that Sharp told us of, and we skirted about to reach the valley where Costello's outfit lay.

No horse tracks showed on the trail we rode. No sound came from anywhere near. There were, of course, birds talking it up in the bushes, and a slow wind that stirred the trees as we rode along. Nothing else but once in a while the rattle of a spur or the creak of a saddle as a horse took strain in climbing, or a rider shifted weight in the saddle. Sunlight dappled the trail with leaf shadows.

We did not talk. We listened as we rode, and from time to time we paused to listen more carefully.

Cap, who was riding point, drew up suddenly, and we closed in around him. Before us was an opening among the branches of the trees lining the trail. Several miles away we could see a green valley, perhaps five hundred feet lower down, and from it sunlight reflected from a window.

"That will be it," Cap commented. "The way Sharp told it, we will be ridin' Costello range at almost any minute."

We pushed on, circling the smaller valleys that made a chain through the hills. Now, from time to time, cattle tracks showed among those of deer and elk.

The ranch, when we came upon it, lay cupped in the hills, a small but comfortable house set back on a green meadow where a stream curled through. There was slow smoke rising from the chimney, and a good lot of horses in the corrals. Sitting on the stoop in front of the house was a man with a rifle across his knees. We saw no other folks around.

In the meadow a dozen or so head of horses were grazing, the sun gleaming from their smooth flanks. It made a handsome sight, but the man on the stoop looked mighty like a guard.

Galloway sat his horse, giving study to the place, and I did likewise. "Looks too easy," Galloway said after a bit. "I don't like it."

"It's a nice morning," Cap commented. "They might just be idling about."

"Or hid out, waiting for us," I said.

We waited, but Judith was impatient. "Flagan, I want to go down there. I want to see Pa."

"You hold off," I said. "You'll see him soon enough . . . when we know it's safe."

"But he may be in danger!" she protested. "They killed my grandfather, you told me so yourself."

"Yes, but it won't ease your pa's mind to have you in their hands, too. You just wait."

The valley where the ranch lay opened into another, wider valley that we could see as we moved along. There were a few cattle in the first one, and we could see more beyond. The grass was green and rich, and running down the streams there was all the snow water that any rancher could want for his stock. Costello had found a good place.

"They're hid out," Galloway said finally. "I have it in mind they're expecting us. No ranch is quiet like that, this time of day. Not with so many men somewhere about."

We had moved along to a lower bench among the trees, a place not forty feet from where the mountain dropped off into the valley. We saw a man come from the ranch house, saw the screen door shut behind him. From where we were, we could hear it slam.

This man, after a few minutes of talk, seated himself on the steps, while the first man went

157

inside, apparently relieved from guard duty.

"Your pa," Cap surmised, "must be in the house. Certain sure, there's something or somebody down there to be watched over."

Nobody was saying what he had been thinking, that it would make little sense to keep Costello alive . . . unless they were worried for fear some neighbor might insist on seeing him. By this time the Fetchens would know about Tom Sharp, a man not likely to be put off, nor one to trifle with. Yet time would be running out.

They might hold Costello as they had planned to hold Judith, one to be used in controlling the other. If Black Fetchen could get hold of Judith, marry her, and so establish legal claim to the Costello ranch, then Costello might be made to disappear, leaving them in control. It was a likely thing, but there was much that was puzzling about the whole affair, and about their possible connection with the Reynolds gang.

We waited under the trees, moving as little as possible, and keeping wary for fear we would be discovered. The whole thing was growing irksome, and Judith had my sympathy. Her pa was down there, and it was natural she would want to see him. Only we needed to know a few more things before we could act against them. We needed to know if Costello was alive, and how they were holding him, and we needed to know what they were after.

By now we were all pretty sure that the cattle had been incidental. They had the Half-Box H herd, and they would try to hold it, but I felt certain there was more to it than the herd, or even the ranch.

We had to wait them out. I knew they were not patient men and would soon tire of lying around in the brush, doing nothing.

"We've got to know more about this setup," I said. "Cap, do you know the story of the Reynolds outfit?"

"No more than everybody hereabouts knows. They gave it out that they were Confederate sympathizers, and began robbin' some gold trains and the like, letting it be known they were gettin' the gold to hold for the South. But most folks thought they had no such idea — not after the gold started pilin' up. They figured they planned to use it for themselves."

"What happened to the gold?"

"I can't say as I ever heard, although no doubt folks who lived round here could tell you."

"Sharp would know," Galloway suggested.

In the fading afternoon the Costello ranch looked mighty pretty. Shadows were stretching out, but down there the light was mellow and lovely. I could see why a man, even a mover like Costello, would like to settle in such a place. And there was good grazing in the hills around.

But we saw nothing of Costello, nor of anyone else at all.

The stars came out and the wind grew cool. Restlessly, I walked out to a place where the valley could be seen in more detail. There were lights in the ranch house, and shadows moved before some of the windows. Suddenly the door opened and someone went in. It was open long enough to admit two or three men.

Judith came up beside me. "Do you think Pa is down there, Flagan?"

"Uh-huh."

She said nothing more for some time, and then wondered out loud, "Why did this happen to us?"

"I reckon folks have wondered that always, Judith. In this case it's no accident, I'm thinking. Your pa or your grandpa knew something somebody else wanted to know, or else for some reason they need this ranch."

"Flagan, I've been thinking about what you wanted to know . . . you know, if Pa had been in Missouri in seventy-one. I am sure he was, because I've just remembered something."

"What?"

"Pa had an uncle who wasn't much good.

He'd gone off and left us after he got into some trouble with the family, and he went out west. Nobody would talk about him much, but he got into more trouble . . . in Denver, I think it was."

"And so?"

"He came back one night. I remember I woke up and heard talking in a low voice, in Pa's side of the tent. I heard another man's voice, a man who sounded odd . . . as if he was sick or something."

That was all she remembered right then, but it was enough to start me thinking.

Maybe what the Costellos knew was nothing they picked up in trade. Maybe it was something that renegade told them that night in Missouri.

That renegade had been in or around Denver. So had Tirey Fletchen. And so had the Reynolds gang.

Chapter 11

We rode away down the mountain to a hollow in the hills, sheltered by overhanging cliffs and a wall of pines, and made camp there where we could have a fire.

"I figure if we go down to the ranch we'll get so shot full of holes our hides wouldn't be worth tanning," Galloway said. "That outfit's all laid out for an ambush, so let's leave 'em wait."

"Seems to me a likely time to be thinkin' of them cattle," Cap suggested.

"Now, there's a good thought. Let's dab a loop on some and check out the brand."

So we settled down over coffee and bacon to consider. It stood to reason that if most of their crowd were waiting for us to show up, there would be only a few watching the cattle, if any at all. In these mountain valleys, with plenty of grass and water, cattle needed no watching.

The upshot of it was that when the sky

lightened with another day coming, we saddled up and went off. The only one who was upset by our decision was Judith.

"This isn't taking me any closer to Pa!" she objected. "I wish I could find a man like Ivanhoe or the Black Knight! He would ride right down there and bring Pa back!"

"You know," I said, "I don't carry any banners for the Fetchen boys, but if the Black Knight was to ride down amongst them in his tin suit he'd have a sieve for an overcoat. Those Fetchens may run short on morals, but morals don't win no turkey-shoots! I know those boys, and they could part your hair with the first bullet and trim around your ears with the next two.

"If you want to choose up heroes to help you, you'd be a sight better off to pick on Robin Hood or Rob Roy. My pa always said you should never walk into a man when he's set for punching. Better to go around him and work him out of balance.

"Well, while they're waiting for us to come down on 'em, we'll simply round up and drive off a few head of cattle. Then we might sort of scout around down to Sharp's place at Buzzard Roost. I'll lay a bet Fetchen has somebody staked out down there to bring him word."

By the time the sun was high we were at

Buzzard Roost and sitting alongside the stove eating crackers and sardines, and I mentioned the Reynolds outfit. I'd scarcely said the name before Sharp was giving us the story.

The Reynolds gang had buried a treasure, some said, somewhere near the Spanish Peaks. They were right over there to the south of us, only a few miles away.

Contrary to what some folks said, they hadn't been a very bloody outfit. Fact was, it was claimed they'd killed nobody in their robberies. Reynolds had some reputation as an outlaw before the war began, and then supposedly he was recruited by the South to loot Colorado of its gold and silver shipments. "There's been a lot of talk about how much he stole," Sharp said, "and how much they buried when the law caught up with them; but no matter what anybody says there's small chance they had over seventy thousand dollars."

"That's a lot," Galloway said, kind of dryly. "That's more money than I'm likely to see in this lifetime."

"Do you think it's there?" Cap asked.

Sharp shrugged. "It's certain they hadn't anything on 'em when they were caught, and they hadn't much time to hide it unless they hid it very soon after taking it — which could be."

Judith wasn't talking, she was just sitting

there looking solemn and kind of scared too, yet knowing her I had a feeling she was scared less for herself than for her Pa. It came to me that I should try, by some trick, to get him away from the ranch.

That was easy said, but the little valley was bounded by pretty high mountains, and getting in and out of such a guarded place would be next to impossible.

Cap drifted off somewhere, and Galloway did, too, while I sat with Judith. I said to her, "Don't you worry. He's all right, and we'll have him out of there in no time."

"Flagan, I just couldn't imagine he would be like this — James Fetchen, I mean."

For a minute I couldn't place James Fetchen, we were so used to calling him Black. Then I said, "How could you know? All you'd seen of him was a tall, fine-looking man riding by on a horse. Believe me, you can't always tell a coyote by his holler. But that Fetchen outfit was known all over the mountains by the trouble they caused, by the shootings and cuttings they'd been in."

Judith left me, to talk with Sharp's wife, and I walked out on the stoop, looking about for Galloway and Cap, but I saw neither one of them. I don't know what made me do it, but I reached my fingers back and slipped the rawhide loop off my six-gun, freeing it for quick use, if need be.

There's times when nothing is more companionable than a six-shooter, and I had an uneasy feeling, almost as if somebody was walking on my grave, or maybe digging one for me.

The sunlight was bright on Buzzard Roost, and on the mountains all around. A dog trotted lazily across the dusty road, and far up the valley I could see cattle feeding on the grass on the lower slopes of Little Sheep. Everything looked peaceful enough.

There seemed no particular reason why I should feel this way just now. Black Fetchen and his kin had reason for wanting to stake out my hide, but it seemed to me they were in no hurry. That outfit was sure of itself. They'd been in shooting scrapes before and they had come out on top, and they figured they would again. Winning can make folks confident . . . or it can make them cautious.

Here and there I'd come out ahead a few times, but it only made me careful. There's too much that can happen — the twig that deflects your bullet just enough, the time you don't quite get the right grasp on the gun butt, the dust that blows in your eyes. . . . Anyway, there's things can happen to the fastest of men and to the best shots. So I was cautious.

And then there's the gun itself. No man in his right mind will play with a gun. I've seen show-offs doing fancy spins and all that. No real gun-fighter ever did. With a hair-trigger, he'd be likely to blow a hole in his belly. The gun-fighter knows enough of guns to be wary of them. He treats them with respect. A pistol was never made for anything except killing, and a gun-fighter never draws a gun unless to shoot, and he shoots to kill. And he doesn't go around trying to gun up a score. That's only done by tin-horns. Nor does he ever notch his gun, another tin-horn trick.

All the while these thoughts were sort of in the back of my mind, I had my eyes searching for a lookout, if there was one. It seemed likely that the Fetchens would have somebody around who could keep a watch on Buzzard's Roost, for anybody coming or going in that country just naturally rode by there, or stopped off.

I gave thought to where I'd hole up if I was to keep a watch on the place. It would be best to find a place on a hillside, or somewhere a man could keep out of sight while seeing all who came and went. That naturally cut down on the possibilities.

I began to feel that somebody was watching me — I could feel it somehow in my bones. Judith, she came out and walked up to me.

"Flagan —" she began, but I cut her off.

"Go back inside," I said. "Take your time, but you get inside and stay there till I come."

"What's wrong?"

"Judith! Damn it, get inside!"

"Flagan Sackett, you can't talk to me like that! Who do you think —"

Sunlight made a slanting light on a gun barrel in the brush not a hundred and fifty feet away. It was a far shot for a six-gun, but I'd hit targets at a greater distance than that.

With my left hand I swept Judith back toward the door, and my right went down for my gun just as the other gun muzzle stabbed flame. It was the movement to push Judith out of the way that saved my bacon, for that bullet whipped by my ear, stinging me as it went.

My six-gun was up and hammering shots. I was holding high because of the distance, and I let three bullets go in one roll of sound, as fast and slick as I could thumb back the hammer and let it drop.

Then I ran forward three steps, and took one to the side and fired again, holding a mite higher because he might be up and running. I was firing at the place I'd seen the flare of the gun muzzle, but was scattering my shots to have a better chance of scoring a hit.

The battering explosion of the shots died

away, leaving a sudden silence, a silence in which the ears cried out for sound. I stood there, gun poised, aware that it was empty, but hesitating to betray the fact to my enemy, whoever he was.

Slowly I lowered the gun muzzle, and as unobtrusively as possible I opened the loading-gate with my thumb and worked the ejector, pushing the empty shell from the cylinder. Instantly, I fed a cartridge into place, then ejected another, and repeated this until the gun was reloaded. In all that time there was no sound, nor was there any movement in the brush.

Unwilling to take my eyes from the brush, I wondered where Cap and Galloway might be.

And had Judith been hit? I felt quite sure she had not, but a body never knew, when there was shooting taking place.

Warily, I took a step toward the brush, but nothing happened.

Off on my right Galloway suddenly spoke. "I think you got him, boy."

Walking slowly toward the brush, I had to make several climbing steps as I got close to it. There was an outcropping of rock, with thick, thorny brush growing around and over it, and several low trees nearby. The whole clump was no more than thirty or forty yards across, and just about as deep.

First thing I saw was the rifle. It was a Henry .44 and there was a fresh groove down the stock, cut by a bullet. There was blood on the leaves, but nothing else.

Gun in hand, I eased into the brush and stood still, listening. It was so quiet I seemed to be hearing my own heart beat. Somewhere off across country a crow cawed; otherwise there was silence. Then the door of the trading post opened and I heard boot heels on the boards.

My eyes scanned the brush, but I could see no sign of anyone there. Parting the branches with my left hand, I stepped past another bush. On a leaf there was a bright crimson spot . . . fresh blood. Just beyond it was a barely visible track of a boot heel in the soft earth. I was expecting a shot at any moment. It was one of those places where a man figures he's being watched by somebody he can't see.

Then I saw a slight reddish smear on the bark of a tree where the wounded man had leaned. He was hit pretty good, it looked like, although a man can sometimes bleed a good bit from a mighty inconsiderable wound.

I could tell that the man I hunted had gone right on through the brush. I followed through and suddenly came to the other side.

For about fifty yards ahead the country was

open, and a quick glance told me that nothing stirred there. Standing under cover of the brush, I began to scan the ground with care, searching every clump of grass or cluster of small rocks – anywhere a man might be concealed.

The ground on this side of the knoll sloped away for several feet, and this place was invisible from the trading post. A man might slip down from the mountain, or come around the base and ease into the brush, leave his horse and get right up to that knoll without anybody being the wiser.

Pistol ready, I walked slowly toward the further trees, my eyes scanning the terrain all around me. Twice I saw flecks of blood.

Beyond the trees, on a small patch of grass, I saw where a horse had been tied on a short rope. By the look of the grass he had been tied there several times, each time feeding close around him. Whoever tied the horse had allowed him just enough rope to crop a little grass without giving him more rope than a man could catch up along with the reins, in one quick move.

Whoever had been watching there must have suddenly decided to try his shot. It must have seemed like a copper-riveted cinch, catching me out like that. Only my move in getting

Judith out of the way had saved me.

Galloway had come up behind me. "You're bleedin', Flagan," he said.

I put my hand to my ear, which had been smarting some, and brought it away bloody. From the feel of it, the bullet had just grazed the top of the ear.

We followed the rider back into the hills a short way, then lost his trail on a dusty stretch. We found no more blood, and from the way he'd moved in going to his horse I figured he hadn't been hurt more than I had been.

When we got back to the trading post, Evan Hawkes was there, making plans with Tom Sharp for the roundup.

It turned out they had friends in common, stock-buyers and the like. There were eight or ten other cattlemen around the country who were all close friends of Sharp, and all of them had come to be wary of the Fetchen boys.

"One thing I want understood," Hawkes said. "This is our fight. They opened the ball, now we're going to play the tune and they'll dance to our music."

"Seems to me you're outnumbered," said Dobie Wiles. He was the hard-bitten foreman of the Slash B. "And it seems to me that JBF Connected brand will cover our brand as well as yours."

"They left blood on the Kansas grass," Galloway said, "blood of the Half-Box H. I figure Hawkes has first call."

He gave a slow grin. "And that includes us."

Chapter 12

The cattle came down from the hills in the morning, drifting ahead of riders from the neighboring ranches. They moved out on the grass of the bottom land and grazed there, while the riders turned again to the hills.

At first only a few riders were to be seen, for the land was rough and there were many canyons. The cowboys moved back into the hills and along the trails and started the cattle drifting down toward the valley.

The chuck wagon was out, and half a dozen local cattlemen, all of whom rode out from time to time only to return and gather near the wagon. James Black Fetchen himself had not appeared, although several Fetchens were seen riding in the hills. Once, Evan Hawkes roped a young steer and, with Tom Sharp as well as two other cattlemen beside him, studied the brand. It was his Half-Box H worked over to a JBF Connected.

"They do better work down in Texas," Breedlove commented. "There's rustlers down there who do it better in the dark."

Rodriguez looked around at Hawkes. "Do you wish to register a complaint, Señor?"

"Let it go. That steer will be wearing a different brand before this is over."

"As you will."

"When this is over, if there is any steer you want to question we can either skin him and check the brand from the reverse side, or turn him into a pool for it to be decided. I want no cattle but my own, and no trouble with anyone but Fetchen."

"And that trouble, Señor — when does it come?"

"I hope to delay it until after the roundup. There's a lot the Fetchens don't know about cattle and rustling. If I figure it right, they're going to come up short and never know what hit them." He glanced around at them. "Gentlemen, this is my fight, mine and the Sackett boys'. There's no reason to get mixed up in it if you don't have to."

"This is our country," Sharp replied, "and we don't take to rustlers. We'll give you all the room you want, but if you need a hand, just lift a yell and we'll be coming."

"Of course, Señor," Rodriguez said mildly, "but there may have to be trouble. A rider from the Fetchen outfit was drinking in Greenhorn. It seems he was not polite to one of my riders. There were seven Fetchens, and my man was alone. At the roundup he will not be alone."

Hawkes nodded. "I know . . . I heard some talk about that, but shooting at a roundup might kill a lot of good men. Let's take it easy and see what happens when the tally is taken."

I listened and had no comment to offer. It was a nice idea, if it worked. It might work, but there were a few outsiders riding with the Fetchen gang now, and they might know more about brand-blotting than the Fetchens did. That scar-faced puncher with the blond hair, for example. What was his name again? . . . Russ Menard.

I spoke the name out loud, and Rodriguez turned on me. *"Russ Menard?* You know him?"

"He's here. He's one of them."

The Mexican's lips tightened, then he bared his teeth in a smile that held no humor. "He is a very bad *hombre*, this Menard. I think no faster man lives when it comes to using the pistol. If he is one of them, there will surely be trouble."

The cattle had scattered so widely in the hills that it was brutally hard work combing them out of the brush and canyons. This was rugged country – canyons, brush, and boulders, with patches of forest, and on the higher slopes thick stands of timber that covered miles. But there was water everywhere, so most of the stock was in good shape. Aside from Hawkes's rustled herd, there were cattle from a dozen other outfits, including those of Tom Sharp. By nightfall several hundred head were gathered in the valley.

Most of the riders were strangers, men from the ranches nearby, good riders and hard-working men. They knew the country and they knew the cattle and so had an advantage over us, who were new to the land. Most of them were Mexicans, and they were some of the best riders and ropers I ever did see. Galloway and me were handy with ropes but in no way as good as most of those around us, who had been using them since they were knee-high to a short pup.

Most of the stock was longhorn, stuff driven in from Texas over the Goodnight Trail. The cattle from New Mexico were of a lighter strain when unmixed with longhorn blood; and there was a shorthorn or whiteface stock brought in from Missouri or somewhere beyond the Mississippi. Both Costello and Sharp had been driving in a few cattle of other breeds, trying to improve their stock to carry more beef.

The longhorn was a good enough beef critter

when he could get enough to eat and drink, but in Texas they might live miles from water, drinking every two or three days, in some cases, and walking off a lot of good beef to get to water.

But in these mountain valleys where there was water a-plenty, there was no need to walk for it and the eastern stock did mighty well. And nowhere did we see the grass all eaten down. There was enough feed to carry more stock than was here.

The only two Fetchens I saw were men I remembered from that day in Tazewell. Their names I didn't learn until I heard them spoken around the roundup fire.

Clyde Fetchen was a wiry man of thirty-five or so with a narrow, tight-lipped look about him. He was a hard worker, which was more than I could say of the others, but not a friendly man by any way of speaking. Len Fetchen was seventeen or eighteen, broad-shouldered, with hair down to his shoulders. He didn't talk at all. Both of them fought shy of Galloway an' me — no doubt told to do so by Black.

Others came to the fire occasionally, but those were the only two I saw. Them and Russ Menard.

Meanwhile we were doing a sight of work

that a body couldn't see around the branding fire. We were doing our work back in the hills, wherever we could find Half-Box H cattle. All their brands had been altered by now, some of the changed brands so fresh the hide was still warm, or almost. Wherever we found them we dabbed a loop over their horns, threw them, and rebranded with a Pig-Pen, which was merely a series of vertical and horizontal lines like several pens side by each. A brand like that could cover everything we found, but we were only hunting stolen Hawkes cattle. We took turn and turn about bringing cattle to the fire, and the rest of the time we roamed up and down the range, sorting out Hawkes cattle.

Russ Menard spent mighty little time working cattle, so he didn't notice what was going on. The Fetchen boys brought in cattle here and there, mostly with their own brand. At night Briggs and Walker could usually manage to cut out a few of them and brand them downwind from the wagon, out of sight in some creek bed or gully.

By the third day half the hands on the range had fallen in with the game and were rebranding the rustled cattle as fast as we were. On the fifth day, James Black Fetchen came riding down from the hills with Russ Menard and six of his riders.

Evan Hawkes was standing by the fire, and when he saw Fetchen coming he called to Ladder Walker. The tall, lean Half-Box H puncher looked up, then slid the thong off his six-gun. The cook took another look, then slipped his shot-gun out of his bed-roll and tucked it in along his dried apples and flour.

Cap Rountree and Moss Reardon were both out on the range, but it so happened I was standing right there, taking time out for coffee.

Fetchen rode on up to the fire and stepped down, and so did Menard and Colby. Fetchen turned his hard eyes to me, then to Walker at the fire. The cook was busy kneading dough. Tom Sharp was there, and so were Rodriguez and Baldwin, who was repping for a couple of outfits over on the Cucharas.

"I want to see the tally list," Fetchen said.

"Help yourself." Hawkes gestured to where it lay on a large rock, held down by a smaller rock.

Fetchen hesitated, and looked hard at Hawkes.

Russ Menard was looking across the fire at me. "You one of them gun-fighting Sacketts?" he asked.

"Never paid gun-fighting no mind," I said.

180

"Too busy making a living. Seems to me a man's got mighty little to do, riding around showing off his gun."

He got kind of red in the face. "Meaning?"

"Meaning nothing a-tall. Just commenting on why I don't figure myself a gun-fighter. We Sacketts never figured on doing any fighting unless pushed," I added.

"What do you carry that gun for?" he demanded.

I grinned at him. "Seems I might meet somebody whose time has come."

Black Fetchen had turned around sharply, his face red and angry. "What the hell is this? You've only got thirty-four head of JBF cattle listed."

"That's all there was," Hawkes said quietly, "and a scrubby lot, too."

Fetchen stepped forward, the color leaving his face, his eyes burning under his heavy brows. "What are you trying to do? Rob me? I came into this valley with more than a thousand head of cattle."

"If you have a bill of sale," Sharp suggested, "we might check out the brands and find out what's wrong. Your bill of sale would show the original brands, and any stolen cattle would have the brands altered."

Fetchen stopped. Suddenly he was cold, dangerous. Me, I was watching Menard.

"You can't get away with this!" Fetchen said furiously.

"If you have any brand you want to question," Sharp said, "we can always shoot the animal and skin it. The inside of the hide will show if the brand has been altered."

Fetchen glanced at him, realizing that to check the brand would reveal the original alteration, the change from Hawkes's Half-Box H to his JBF Connected. Frustrated, he hesitated, suddenly aware he had no way to turn.

Hawkes, Sharp, and Rodriguez were scattered out. Baldwin stood near the chuck wagon, and all of them were armed. Ladder Walker had released the calf he had been branding and was now standing upright, branding iron in his left hand.

And there was me.

To start shooting now would mean death for several men, and victory for nobody. Fetchen started to speak, then his eye caught the dull gloss of the shotgun stock, inches from the cook's hand.

"While we're talking," I suggested, "you might tell Costello he should be down here, repping for his brand. We have business to discuss with him."

182

"He's not well," Fetchen replied, controlling his anger. "I'll speak for him."

"Costello is a very good friend of mine," Sharp said, "and a highly respected man in this country. We want to be sure he stays well. I think he should be brought down to my place where he can have the attention of a doctor."

"He's not able to ride," Fetchen said. He was worried now, and eager to be away. Whatever his plans had been, they were not working now. His herd was gone, taken back by the very man from whom it had been stolen, and the possibility of his remaining in the area and ranching was now slim indeed.

"Load him into a wagon," Sharp insisted. "If you don't have one, I'll send one up, and enough men to load him up."

Fetchen backed off. "I'll see. I'll talk to him," he said.

Right at that moment I figured him for the most dangerous man I'd ever known. There'd been talk about his hot temper, but this man was cold — cold and mean. You could see it in him, see him fighting down the urge to grab for a gun and turn that branding fire into a blaze of hell. He had it in him, too, only he was playing it smart. And a few moments later I saw another reason why.

Moss Reardon, Cap Rountree, and Galloway had come up behind us, and off to the left was Kyle Shore.

Fetchen's gang would have cut some of us down, but not a one of them would have escaped.

Russ Menard looked at me and smiled. "We'll meet up, one of these days."

"We can make it right now," I said. "We can make it a private fight."

"I ain't in no hurry."

James Black Fetchen looked past me toward the chuck wagon. "Judith, your pa wants you. You comin'?"

"No."

"You turnin' your back on him?"

"You know better than that. When he comes down to Mr. Sharp's, at Buzzard Roost, I'll be waiting for him."

The Fetchens went to their horses then, Russ Menard taking the most time. When he was in the saddle, both hands out in plain sight, he said, "Don't you disappoint me, boy. I'll be hunting you."

They rode away, and Tom Sharp swore softly. With the back of his hand, he wiped sudden sweat from his forehead. "I don't want to go through that again. For a minute there, anything could have happened."

"You sleep with locked doors," Galloway said, riding up. "And don't answer no hails by night. That's a murdering lot."

The rest of the roundup went forward without a hitch. The cattle were driven in from the hills and we saw no more of the Fetchens, but Costello did not come down from the hills. Twice members of the gang were seen close to the Spanish Peaks. Once several of them rode over to Badito.

The roundup over, Rodriguez announced a fandango. That was their name for a big dancing and to-do, where the folks come from miles around. Since no rider from the Fetchen crowd had come down to claim the beef that still wore their brand over the Half-Box H, it was slaughtered for a barbecue . . . at least, the three best steers were.

Rodriguez came around to Galloway and me. "You will honor my house, Señores? Yours is a name well known to me. Tyrel Sackett is married to the daughter of an old friend of mine in New Mexico."

"We will come," I said.

Nobody talked much of anything else, and Galloway and me decided we'd ride down to Pueblo or up to Denver to buy us new outfits. Judith was all excited, and was taking a hand in the planning.

We rode off to Denver, and it was two weeks before we got back, just the night of the big shindig. The first person we saw was Cap Rountree.

"You didn't come none too soon," he said. "Harry Briggs is dead . . . dry-gulched."

Chapter 13

It had been a particularly vicious killing. Not only had Briggs been shot from ambush, but his killers had ridden over his body and shot into it again and again.

There could be no doubt as to why it had been done. Briggs was a hard-working cowhand with no enemies, and he carried no money; of the little he could save, the greater part was sent to a sister in Pennsylvania. He had been killed because he rode for the Half-Box H, and it could just as easily have been any of the other hands.

And there was no doubt as to who had done it, though there didn't seem to be any chance of proving it. It was the Fetchen crowd, we knew. There was no other possibility. From the fragments of tracks found near the body, they could tell that more than one killer was involved; he had been shot with at least two different weapons — probably more.

"We've done some scoutin' around," Reardon told us. "The Fetchen riders have been huntin' around the Spanish Peaks. We found tracks up that way. Sharp figures they're huntin' the Reynolds treasure."

Ladder Walker was glum. "Briggs was a good man. Never done harm to nobody. I'm fixin' to hunt me some Fetchens."

"Take it easy," Reardon warned. "Those boys are mean, and they ain't about to give you no chance. No fair chance, that is."

Judith was standing on the porch when I rode up. "Flagan, I'm worried about Pa. All this time, and no word. Nobody has seen him, and the Fetchens won't let anyone come near the place."

I'd been giving it considerable thought, and riding back from Denver, Galloway and me had made up our minds to do something about it. The trouble was, we didn't know exactly what.

Nobody in his right mind goes riding into a bottle-necked valley where there's fifteen to twenty men waiting for him, all fixing to notch their guns for his scalp. And the sides of the valley allowed for no other approach we knew of. Yet there had to be a way, and one way might be to cause some kind of diversion.

"Suppose," I suggested, "we give it out that

we've found some sign of that Reynolds gold? We could pick some lonely place over close to Spanish Peaks, let out the rumor that we had it located and were going in to pick it up."

"With a big enough party to draw them all away from the ranch?"

"That's right. It wouldn't do any harm, and it might pull them all away so we could ride in and look around."

We finally picked on a place not so far off as the Spanish Peaks. We rode over to Bandito — Galloway, Ladder Walker, and me — and we had a couple of drinks and talked about how we'd located the Reynolds treasure.

Everybody for miles around had heard that story, so, like we figured, there were questions put to us. "Is it near the Spanish Peaks?" one man asked.

"That's just it," Galloway said. "Everybody took it for granted that when Reynolds talked about twin peaks he meant the Spanish Peaks. Well, that was where everybody went wrong. The peaks Reynolds and them talked about were right up at the top of the Sangre de Cristos. I mean what's called Blanca Peak."

"There's three peaks up there," somebody objected.

"Depends on where you stand to look at

them. I figure that after they buried the loot they took them for landmarks — just looked back and saw only two peaks, close together."

"So you think you've found the place?" The questioner was skeptical. "So have a lot of others."

"We found a knife stuck into a tree for a marker, and we found a stone slab with markings on it."

Oh, we had them now. Everybody knew that Reynolds had told of thrusting a knife into a tree to mark the place, so we knew our story would be all around the country in a matter of hours. Somebody would be sure to tell the Fetchens, just to get their reaction.

"We're going up there in the morning," Walker said, making out to be drunker than he was. "We'll camp in Bronco Dan Gulch, and we'll be within a mile of the treasure. You just wait. Come daylight, we'll come down the pass loaded with gold."

Now, Bronco Dan was a narrow little gulch that headed up near the base of Lone Rock Hill, only three or four miles from the top of the rim. It was wild country, and just such a place as outlaws might choose to hide out or cache some loot. And it wasn't but a little way above La Veta Pass.

Anyway a body looked at it, the place made a

lot of sense. La Veta Pass was the natural escape route for anybody trying to get over the mountains from Walsenburg to Alamosa, and vice versa.

Of course, they knew about the knife. That was the common feature of the stories about the Reynolds treasure — that he had marked the place by driving a knife into a tree. The stone marker was pure invention, but they found it easy to accept the idea that Reynolds might have scratched a map on a slab of rock.

That night Cap Rountree went up the mountain and hid in the brush where he could watch the Costello place, and when we arrived shortly after daybreak he told us the Fetchens had taken out in a pack just before daylight.

"They took the bait, all right. Oh, yes, I could see just enough to see them ride out."

"How many stayed behind?"

"Two, three maybe. I don't know for sure."

Galloway went to his horse, and I did the same. You can lay a couple of bets I wasn't anxious to go down there, but we had set this up and this was the chance we'd been playing for.

Cap started to follow along, but I waved him back. "You stay here. No use all of us getting boxed in down there. If you see them coming back, give a shout."

Ladder Walker was along with us — there was no leaving him out of it. So the three of us went down the mountain, following the trail where cattle had crossed a saddle, and we came into the valley within two hundred yards of the ranch, just beyond the corral.

"Stay with the horses, Ladder," I said. "And keep an eye on the opening. I don't like this place, not a bit."

"You figure it for a trap?"

"Could be. Black Fetchen is a wily one, and we've had it too easy so far. We've had almost too much luck."

Galloway and me, spread apart a little, walked toward the house.

We played it in luck this time too. Nobody seemed to be around until we stepped up on the porch. Then we could hear voices coming from the back of the house.

"Don't get any ideas, old man. You just set tight until the boys come back. Then maybe Black will let you go. If'n he can find that gold and them Sacketts all to once, he might come back plumb satisfied."

"He won't find the Sacketts," I said, stepping from the hallway into the room where they sat. It was the kitchen, and on my sudden entrance one of the men stood up so quick he almost turned over the table.

"Get your hat, Mr. Costello," I said. "We've come to take you to Judith."

I hadn't drawn my gun, being of no mind to shoot anybody unless they asked for it. There were two of Fetchen's men in the room and our arriving that way had taken the wind out of them. They just looked at us, even the one who had stood up so quick.

Costello, who was a slim, oldish man with a shock of graying hair, got up and put on his hat.

"Here, now!" The Fetchen man standing up had gotten his senses back, and he was mad. "Costello, you come back and set down! The same goes for you Sacketts, unless you want to get killed. Black Fetchen is ridin' up to this ranch right now."

"We needn't have any trouble," I said calmly.

"I'll get a horse," Galloway said, and ducked out of the door, Costello following him.

"Black will kill you, Sackett. He'll fill your hide with lead."

"I doubt if he's got the guts to try. You tell him I said that."

"I hear tell you're a fast man with a shootin' iron." I could just see the gambler stirring around inside him, and it looked as if it was gettin' the better of his common sense. "I don't think we need to wait for Black. I'd sort of like to try you on myself."

"Your choice."

Meanwhile I walked on into the room, and right up to him. Now, no man likes to start a shooting match at point-blank range, because skill plays mighty little part in it then, and the odds are that both men will get blasted. And anyhow, nobody in his right mind starts shooting at all unless there's no other way, and I wasn't planning on shooting now, if I could help it.

So I just walked in on him and he backed off a step, and when he started to take another step back, I hit him. It was the last thing he was expecting, and the blow knocked him down. It was one quick move for me to slip his gun from its holster and straighten up, but the other man hadn't moved.

"You shuck your guns," I told him. "You just unbuckle and step back, and be careful how you move your hands. I'm a man mighty subject to impressions, and you give me the wrong one and I'm likely to open you up like a gutted sheep."

"I ain't figurin' on it. You just watch it, now." He moved his hands with great care to his belt buckle, unhitched, and let the gun belt fall.

The man on the floor was sitting up. "What's

the matter, you yella?" he said to his companion.

"I'm figurin' on livin' a mighty long time, that's all. I ain't seen a gray hair yet, and I got my teeth. Anyway, I didn't see you cuttin' much ice."

"I should've killed him."

"You done the right thing, to my thinkin'. Maybe I ain't so gun-slick as some, and maybe I ain't so smart, but I sure enough know when to back off from a fire so's not to get burned. Don't you get no fancy notions now, Ed. You'd get us both killed."

Well, I gathered up those guns and a rifle I saw in the corner by the door, then I just backed off.

Galloway and Costello were up in their saddles, holding my horse ready.

There wasn't any move from the house until we were cutting around the corral toward the trail down which we had come, and then one man ran from the house toward the barn. Glancing back, I was just in time to see him come out with a rifle, but he took no aim at us; he just lifted the rifle in one hand and fired two quick shots, a space, and then a third shot . . . and he was firing into the air.

"Trouble!" I yelled. "That was a signal!"

Ladder Walker, who had hung back, wanting

a shot at anyone who had helped to kill Briggs, now came rushing up behind us. The trail to the saddle over which he had come into the valley was steep, and a hard scramble for the horses, but much of it was among the trees and partly concealed from below.

We heard a wild yell from below and, looking back, I saw Black Fetchen, plainly recognizable because of the horse he rode, charging into the valley, followed by half a dozen riders.

Even as I looked, a man ran toward him, pointing up the mountain. Instantly there was firing, but shooting uphill is apt to be a tricky thing even for a skilled marksman, and their bullets struck well behind us. Before they had the range we were too far away for them, and they wasted no more shots.

But they were coming after us. We could hear their horses far below, and saw the men we had caught in the house catching up horses at the corral, ready to follow.

Deliberately, Galloway slowed his pace. "Easiest way to kill a horse," he said, "running it uphill. We'll leave that to them."

Riding close to Costello, I handed him the gun belt and rifle I'd taken from the cabin. When I'd first run out I had slung the belt over the pommel and hung onto the rifle.

Up ahead of us we heard the sudden boom of

a heavy rifle . . . Cap Rountree and his buffalo gun. A moment later came a second shot. He was firing a .56 Spencer that carried a wicked wallop. Personally, I favored the Winchester .44, but that big Spencer made a boom that was a frightening thing to hear, and it could tear a hole in a man it hit so that it was unlikely a doctor would do him much good.

Cap was in the saddle when we reached him, but he made us pull up. "Flagan," he said, "I don't like the look of it. Where's the rest of them?"

There were six or seven behind us, that we knew, but what of the rest?

"You figure we're trapped?" I asked.

"You just look at it. They must know how we got up here, and they can ride out their gap and block our way down the mountain before we can get there."

I was not one to underrate Black Fetchen. Back at the Costello place that man had said Fetchen was due to come riding in at any moment, and at the time I gave it no credit, figuring he was trying a bluff, but then some of the outfit had showed up.

Ladder Walker turned his mount and galloped to a spot where he could look over part of the trail up which we had come in first arriving at our lookout point. He was back in an instant. "Dust down there. Somebody is movin' on the trail."

"Is there a trail south, toward Bronco Dan?"

Cap Rountree chewed his mustache. "There's a shadow of a trail down Placer Creek to La Veta Pass, but that's where you sent some of this outfit. Likely the Fetchens know that trail. If you try it, and they're waitin', it's a death trap."

I gave a glance up toward those peaks that shut us off from the west, and felt something like fear. It was almighty icy and cold up there against the sky, up there where the timber ran out and the raw-backed ridges gnawed the sky. My eyes went along the east face of those ridges.

"What about west?" I asked.

"Well," Cap said reluctantly, "there's a pass off north called Mosca Pass. It's high up and cold, and when you come down the other side you're in the sand dunes."

"We got a choice?" Galloway asked.

"Either run or fight," Walker said, "and if we fight we'll be outnumbered three or four to one."

"I like the odds," Galloway said, "but somebody among us will die."

I looked over at Costello. "Do you know that pass?"

"I know it. If there's any trail there from here,

it's nothing but a sheep trail."

"Let's go," I said. Below us we could hear them coming – in fact, we could hear them on both trails.

Costello led off, knowing the country best. Cap knew it by hearsay, but Costello had been up to the pass once, coming on it from the ancient Indian trail that led down Aspen Creek.

We started up the steep mountainside covered with trees, and followed a sort of trail made by deer or mountain sheep.

Mosca Pass had been the old Indian route across the mountains. Later it had been used by freighters, but now it was used only by occasional horsemen who knew the country, and sheepherders bringing their flocks to summer grazing.

Beyond the pass, on the western side, lay the great sand dunes, eighty square miles of shifting, piled-up sand, a place haunted by mystery, avoided by Indians, and a place I'd heard talk of ever since entering Colorado, because of the mysterious disappearances of at least one train of freight wagons and a flock of a thousand sheep, along with the herder.

We didn't have any choice. Black Fetchen undoubtedly had gone himself or had sent riders to look into the story of the Reynolds gold, but at the same time he'd kept riders close to Costello's place to move in if we tried to rescue him. I thought the only thing they hadn't guessed was the trail down the mountain from the saddle. Their missing that one was enough to get us a chance to free Costello; but now they were pushing us back into the mountains, leaving us mighty little room in which to maneuver.

The ridge along which we now rode was a wall that would shut us in. We had to try for one of the passes, and if we succeeded in getting across the mountain we would be on the edge of the sand dunes.

Suppose Black could send those riders who had gone to Bronco Dan Gulch on through La Veta Pass? They could close in from the south, and our only way of escape would be into the dunes. It began to look as if we were fairly trapped, cornered by our own trick, trying to get rid of the gang for a few hours.

From time to time we had to shift our trail. Sometimes it simply gave out, or the ground fell away too steep for any horse to travel. There was no question of speed. Our horses sometimes slid down hill as much as ten to twenty feet, and at times the only thing that saved us were outcroppings of rock or the stands of pine growing on the slope.

But most of the way was under cover and

there was no chance of dust, so anybody trying to track us could not be sure exactly where we were.

"We could hole up and make a stand," Walker suggested.

"They'd get above us," Galloway said. "They'd have us trapped on a steep slope so we couldn't go up or down."

Once, breaking out of the timber, we glimpsed the smoke rising from the trading post near the Buzzard Roost Ranch. It was miles away, and there was no chance of us getting down there without breaking through a line of guns. We could make out riders below us, traveling on the lower slopes, cutting us off.

Suddenly there was a bare slope before us, a slope of shale. It was several hundred yards across and extended down the mountain for what must be a quarter of a mile.

Galloway, who was in the lead at the moment, pulled up and we gathered near him. "I don't like it, Flagan," he said. "If that shale started to slide, a man wouldn't have a chance. It would take a horse right off its feet."

We looked up, but the slope above was steep and rocky. A man afoot could have made it with some struggling here and there, but there was no place a horse could go. And downhill was as bad . . . or worse.

"Ain't much of a choice," Cap said.

"I'll try it," I said. Even as I spoke I was thinking what a fool a man could be. If we tried going back we'd surely run into a shooting match and somebody would get killed — maybe all of us — but if my horse started to slide on that shale I'd surely go all the way; and it was so steep further down that the edge almost seemed to break off sharply.

Stepping down from the saddle, I started toward the edge of the slope, but my horse wanted no part of it. He pulled back, and I had to tug hard to get him out on that shale.

At my first step I sank in over my ankle, but I didn't slide. Bit by bit, taking it as easy as I could, I started out over the slide area. I was not halfway across when I suddenly went in almost to my knees. I struggled to get my feet out of the shale, and felt myself starting to slide. Holding still, I waited a moment, and then I could ease a foot from the shale and managed a step forward. It was harder for my horse, but a good hold on the reins gave him confidence and he came on across the stretch. It took me half an hour to get to the other side, but I made it, though twice my horse went in almost to his belly.

It was easier for the next man, who was Cap Rountree. Cap had been watching me, and I had found a few almost solid places I could point out to him. Before he was across, Walker started, then Costello. All told, that slide held us up a good two hours, but once across we found ourselves on a long, narrow bench that carried us on for over a mile, moving at a good gait.

The top of the pass was open, wind-swept and cold. The western side of it fell steeply away before us. Hesitating, we looked back and glimpsed a bunch of riders, still some miles off, but riding up the pass toward us.

Black Fetchen had planned every move with care. Now we could see just how he must have thought it out, and it mattered not at all whether he went to Bronco Dan or not, he could have trapped us in any case. I was sure they had sent up a smoke or signaled in some manner, and that when we reached the foot of the pass he would have men waiting for us.

The others agreed, so we hunched our shoulders against the chill wind and tried to figure a way out.

It looked as if we either had to fight, facing enemies on both sides, or we had to take our chances in the waterless waste of the sand dunes.

Black Fetchen had taken setbacks and had waited; and then, like a shrewd general, he had boxed us in.

Harry Briggs was dead . . . murdered. And now it would be us, trapped in the dunes where the sand would cover our bodies. And then Fetchen could go back to get the others . . . to get Evan Hawkes and his men.

To get Judith. . . .

Chapter 14

Galloway urged his horse close to mine and pointed down the mountain. "Riders coming!" he said.

There were two of them, out in the open and coming at a good clip, considering they were riding uphill. We could not make out who they were, but they came on, and no shots were fired.

When they topped out on the ridge we saw they were Kyle Shore and Moss Reardon.

"There's been a shooting over at Greenhorn," Kyle said. "Black Fetchen killed Dobie Wiles in a gun battle — an argument over cattle."

"You boys have ridden right into a trap," Walker told them. "The Fetchens have us boxed in."

They looked around, seeing nobody. "You sure?"

"We'd better get off the ridge," Galloway

advised. "Here we're sitting ducks."

"We didn't see anybody," Reardon said doubtfully.

"Try going back," Cap told him. "They're out there, all right."

So now Dobie, foreman of the Slash B, and an outspoken enemy of the Fetchens, was dead. Whatever had brought the Fetchens into this country, it was an all-out war now.

Pushing my horse to the lead, I rode over the rim and started down the steep trail toward the dunes. As I rode, I was trying to figure some way out of this corner without a fight. Not that I was dodging a fight with the Fetchens. That had to come, but right now the odds were all against us and nobody wants to begin a fight he stands to lose. What I wanted was to find a place we could fight from that would come close to evening things up.

"Keep your eyes skinned," I said over my shoulder. "Unless I've got it wrong, there'll be more Fetchens coming in from the south."

Galloway looked back up the mountain. "They're up there, Flagan," he said, "right on the rim."

Sure enough, we could count eight or nine, and knew there were twice that many close by.

"Flagan," Cap said, "look yonder!"

He pointed to a dust cloud a couple of miles

off to the south, a dust cloud made by hard-ridden horses.

It looked to me as if we were up the creek without a paddle, because not far below us the trees scattered out and the country was bare all around, with no kind of shelter. We'd have to stand and fight, or run for the dunes. Well, I just pulled up, stopping so short they all bunched in around me.

"I'll be damned if we do!" I said.

"Do what? What d'you mean?"

"Look at it. He's heading us right into those dunes. We could get boxed in there and die of thirst, or maybe he's got a couple of boys perched on top of one of those dunes with rifles. Just as we get close to them, they'd open fire."

Riders were now on the trail behind us, but some distance back.

"What do you figure to do?"

"We've got to get off this trail. We've got to make our own way, not ride right down the trail he's got set for us."

We walked our horses on through the trees, searching for some kind of way we could take to get off the trail. Knowing the ways of wild game, we figured there might be some trail along the mountainside. Of course, a man on horseback can't follow a deer trail very far

207

unless he's lucky, the way we had been earlier. A deer will go under tree limbs, over rocks, or between boulders where no horse could go. We scattered about as much as the trail and the terrain would allow, and we hunted for tracks.

We were under cover now, out of view from both above and below, but that would not last long.

Ladder Walker came back up the trail from where he had scouted. "They're closin' in, Flagan. They'll be under cover an' waitin' when we show up."

The forest and the mountains have their own secret ways, and in the changing of days the seemingly changeless hills do also change. Fallen snow settles into crevices in the rock and expands in freezing, and so cracks the rock still further. Wind, rain, and blown sand hone the edges of the jagged upthrusts of rocks, and find the weak places to hollow them away.

In the passing of years the great cliffs crumble into battlements with lower flanks of talus, scattered slopes of rock, and debris fallen from the crumbling escarpment above.

There upon the north side of the trail I saw a fallen pine, its roots torn from the earth and leaning far over, exposing a narrow opening through the thick timber and the rocks into a glade beyond. It might be no more than a dead end, but it was our only chance, and we took it.

Swiftly, I turned my horse up into the opening, scrambling around the roots, and down through the narrow gap beyond into the glade.

"Cap, you and Moss fix up that trail, will you? We're going to need time."

Maybe we had run into an even worse trap, but at least it was a trap of our own making, not one set and waiting for us. A blind man could sense that Black Fetchen was out for a kill. He did not want just Galloway and me, although no doubt we topped his list: he wanted us all.

While we held up, waiting for Cap and Moss to blot out our trail, I scouted around.

There was a narrow aisle among the pines that followed along the slope toward the north. A body could see along it for fifty or sixty yards. When Cap and Moss came up, we pushed on.

We rode on no trail except one we made, and we found our way with difficulty, weaving among trees and rocks, scrambling on steep slopes, easing down declivities where our horses almost slid on their hind quarters. Suddenly we came upon a great slash on the mountain, came upon it just where it ended.

A huge boulder had torn loose hundreds of feet up the mountain and had come tumbling down, crushing all before it, leaving a steep but natural way toward the higher slopes.

Costello glanced up the mountain. "We'll never make it," he said, seeing my look. "It's too steep."

"We'll get down and walk," I said. "We'll lead our horses. It's going to be a scramble, but it'll be no easier for those who follow, and we'll have the advantage of being above them."

Swinging down, I led off. Mostly it was a matter of finding a way around the fallen trees and rocks, scrambling up slopes, pushing brush or fallen trees out of the way. In no time at all we were sweating, fighting for breath from the work and the altitude.

We were topping out at the head of our long corridor when Ladder kind of jerked in the saddle and gave an odd grunt. Almost at the same instant, we heard the shots.

We saw them at once. They were below us, in the open beyond some trees. They had lost our trail until we came into sight on the slope, and they had fired . . . from a good four hundred yards off.

Scrambling into the trees, I swung around on Ladder. "You hurt?"

"I caught one. You boys keep going. I can handle this."

"Like hell." I got down.

Cap and Galloway had already moved to the

edge of the trees and were returning the searching fire the Fetchens were sending into the trees. We had bullets all around us, but most of them were hitting short ... shooting up or down hill is always a chancy thing.

Ladder Walker had caught a .44 slug on the hip bone — a glancing shot that hit the bone and turned off, tearing a nasty gash in the flesh. It was not much more than a flesh wound, but he was losing blood.

We made a sort of pad with a patch of moss ripped from a tree trunk, binding it in place with his torn shirt.

We were under cover now, and our return fire had made them wary, so with Walker sitting his saddle, we worked our way along the slope and across Buck Creek Canyon.

There was nothing about this that a man could like. We had broken the trap, but we were far from free. They were wasting no shots, moving in carefully, determined to make an end of us. We had them above and below us, others closing in, and no doubt some trying to head us off.

Pulling up suddenly, I stood in my stirrups and looked off down through the trees toward the sand dunes. If they tried to follow along the side of the mountain below us, we might be able to drive them into the dunes.

Cap rode up beside me. "Flagan, there's a creek somewhere up ahead that cuts through the mountain, or nearly so. I figure if we could get up there we could ride up the creek and cross the mountain; then we could come down behind the Buzzard Roost ranch."

We moved along, taking our time, hunting out a trail as we rode. There was a good smell of pines in the air, and overhead a fine blue sky with white clouds that were darkening into gray, sort of bunching up as if the Good Lord was getting them corralled for a storm.

The traveling was easier now. We wound in and out amongst the fallen trees, most of them long dead, and the boulders that had tumbled down from the mountain higher up. The ground was thick with pine needles or moss, and there were some damp places where water was oozing out.

For about half a mile we had cover of a sort. We couldn't see any of the Fetchen gang, nor could they shoot at us, but there was no chance to make time. Had we slipped from their trap, maybe only to get into a worse one, I wondered. We all rode with our Winchesters in our hands, ready for the trouble we knew was shaping up.

On our right the mountains rose steeply for more than two thousand feet, their peaks hidden in the dark clouds. The air grew still, and the few birds we saw were flying low, hunting cover. A few scattering drops of rain fell.

There came a puff of wind, and then a scattering shower, and we drew up to get into our slickers. The grass on the mountain slope seemed suddenly greener, the pines darker.

Glancing at Ladder Walker, I saw he looked almighty drawn and pale. He caught my eyes and said, "Don't you worry your head, Sackett. I'm riding strong."

It was no easy place to travel. Because the mountainside was so steep we had to pick our way carefully, stopping from time to time to give the horses a breathing spell. We were angling up again now, hunting for the cover of scattered trees that showed higher up. Thunder rumbled back in the peaks, sounding like great boulders tumbling down a rocky corridor. Lightning flashed, giving a weird light.

Galloway, who was riding point at the moment, caught the movement of a man as he was lifting his rifle, and Galloway was not one to waste time. He shot right off his saddle, his rifle held waist-high . . . and nobody ever lived who was better at off-hand shooting than Galloway.

We heard a yelp of pain, then the clatter of a rifle falling among rocks; and then there was a burst of firing and we left our saddles as if we'd been shot from them. We hit ground running and firing, changing position as we hit grass, and all shooting as soon as we caught sight of something to shoot.

They'd caught us in the open, on the slope of a rock-crested knoll crowned with trees. We were short a hundred yards or so of the trees, but Cap and Galloway made the knoll and opened a covering fire. Costello helped Walker to a protected spot, whilst Moss and me gathered the horses and hustled them behind the knoll.

We stood there a moment, feeling the scattering big drops before an onrush of rain. The back of that knoll fell away where a watercourse made by mountain runoff had cut its way. There was shelter here for the horses, but there was a covered route down to the next canyon.

"They aren't about to rush us," I told Moss. "You stay here with the horses. I'm going down this gully to see if we can get out of here."

"You step careful boy," Reardon said. "Them Fetchens have no idea of anybody getting home alive."

The Fetchens were going to be wary, and all the more so because they probably figured they'd either killed or wounded some of us when we left our saddles like that. Now they were getting return fire from only two rifles, with occasional shots from Costello, so they would be sure they were winning and had us nailed down.

Rifle in hand, I crept down that gully, sliding over wet boulders and through thick clumps of brush. All the time I was scouting a route down which we could bring our horses as well as ourselves.

Suddenly, from up above, a stick cracked. Instantly I froze into position, my eyes moving up slope. A man was easing along through the brush up there, his eyes looking back the way I had come. It seemed as if the Fetchens were closing in around my friends, and there wasn't much I could do about it.

Going back now was out of the question, so I waited, knowing a rifle shot would alert them to trouble up here. When that man up there moved again . . . He moved.

He was a mite careless because he didn't figure there was anybody so far in this direction, and when he moved I put my sights on him and held my aim, took a long breath, let it out, and squeezed off my shot. He was moving when I fired, but I had taken that into account, and my bullet took him right through the ribs.

He straightened up, held still for a moment, and then fell, head over heels down the slope, ending up within twenty feet of me.

Snaking through the brush, I got up to him and took his gun belt off him and slung it across my shoulders. Also taking up his rifle, I aimed it on the woods up above, where there were likely some others, and opened fire.

It was wild shooting, but I wanted to flush them out if I could, and also wanted to warn my folks back there that it was time to get out.

There were nine shots left in the Winchester, and I dusted those woods with them; then I threw down the rifle and slipped back the way I had come. A few shots were fired from somewhere up yonder, fired at the place from which I'd been shooting but I was fifty yards off by that time and well down in the watercourse where I'd been traveling.

Waiting and listening, it was only minutes until I heard movement behind me and, rifle up, I held ready for trouble.

First thing I saw was Moss Reardon. "Hold your fire, boy," he said. "It's us a-comin'."

Me, I went off down the line and brought up on the edge of a small canyon; it was no trouble to get down at that point. When the others bunched around, I pointed down canyon. "Yonder's the dunes. And there seems to be a creek running along there. I take it we'd better reach for the creek and sort of take account of things."

"Might be Medano Creek," Cap said.

"What's that amount to?"

"If it's Medano, we can foller it up and over the divide. I figure it will bring us out back in the hills from Buzzard Roost."

Once more in the saddle, I led off down the canyon, and soon enough we were under the cottonwoods and willows, with a trickle of water at our feet. There was a little rain falling by then, and lightning playing tag amongst the peaks.

Ladder seemed to be in bad shape. He was looking mighty peaked. He'd lost a sight of blood, and that crawling and sliding hadn't done him any good.

The place we'd come to had six-foot banks, and there was a kind of S bend in the stream that gave us the shelter of banks on all sides. Just beyond were the dunes. From a high point on the bank we could see where the creek came down out of the Sangre de Cristos.

"We might as well face up to it," Galloway said. "We're backed up against death. Those boys are downstream of us and they're up on the mountain, and they surely count us to be dead before nightfall."

"One of them doesn't. I left him stretched out up yonder. This here's his gun belt."

"One less to carry a rifle against us," Moss said. He leaned back against the bank. "Gol durn it. I ain't as young as I used to be. This scramblin' around over mountains ain't what I'm trimmed for. I'm a horse-and-saddle man myself."

"I'd walk if I could get out of here," Galloway said.

Costello was saying nothing. He was just lying yonder looking all played out. He was no youngster, and he'd been mistreated by the Fetchens. So we had a wounded man and one in no shape to go through much of this traveling, and we were a whole mountain away from home.

That Medano Creek might be the way, but I didn't like the look of it. It opened up too wide by far for safety.

"Make some coffee, somebody," I suggested. "They know already where we are."

Moss dug into his war-bag for the coffee and I poked around, picking up brush and bark to build us a fire. It took no time at all to have water boiling and the smell of coffee in the air. We had a snug enough place for the moment, with some shelter from gunfire, and water as we needed it.

Galloway and Cap had gone to work to rig a lean-to shelter for Ladder Walker.

There were willow branches leaning out from the bank and they wove other branches among them until they had the willows leaning down and making a kind of roof for those who would lie down. Where the creek curved around there were two or three big old cottonwoods and we bunched the horses there.

We sat around, shoulders bent against the rain, gulping hot coffee and trying to figure what we were going to do.

The Fetchens had us bunched for the kill. They were good mountain fighters, and they had herded us right into a corner. Maybe we could ride up Medano Creek and get clean away, but it looked too inviting to me. It would be a death trap if they waited for us up there where the cliffs grew high.

If we got out of this alive we'd have to be lucky. We'd have to be hung with four-leaf clovers – and I couldn't see any clover around here.

Chapter 15

The worst of it was, we weren't getting much of a look at those boys. They were playing it safe, slipping about in the trees and brush as slick as Comanches.

"Galloway," I said, "I'm getting sort of peevish. Seems to me we've let those boys have at us about long enough. A time comes when a man just can't side-step a fight no longer. We've waited for them to bring it to us, and they've done no such thing, so I figure it's up to you and me to take it to them."

"You give me time for another cup of coffee," Galloway said, "and I'll come along with you."

Cap Rountree looked at us thoughtfully. "What you expect *us* to do . . . mildew?"

Me, I just grinned at him. "Cap, I know you're an old he coon from the high-up hills, but the fewer we have out there the better. You boys can stay right here. They'll be expecting us to move on pretty quick, and they'll be settled down waiting for it. Well, me and Galloway figure to stir them up a mite.

"Anyway," I went on, "Ladder's in no shape to travel more'n he's going to have to, getting out of here. Costello's in pretty bad shape, too. I figure you and Moss can hold this place if they try to attack you, which I doubt they will."

Galloway and me, we picked up our rifles and just sort of filtered back into the brush. "You thinking the same thing I am?" I said.

"Their horses?"

"Uh-huh. If we set them afoot we've got a free ride . . . after we get through that valley yonder."

We'd been timber-raised, like most Tennessee mountain boys, so when we left our horses we swapped our boots for moccasins, which we always carried in our saddlebags.

The weather was clouded up again and it was likely to rain at any moment. We found no sign of the Fetchens until I came upon a corn-shuck cigarette lying on the moss near the butt end of a fallen tree. It was dry, so it must have been dropped since the last shower. After scouting around we found tracks, and then we worked our way up the mountain, moving all the quieter because of the rain-soaked ground.

Suddenly, high up on the mountain, there was a shot.

A voice spoke so close we both jumped in our skins. "Now what the hell was *that?*"

Galloway and me froze where we stood. The speaker couldn't be much more than twenty feet off from us.

"Do you s'pose one of them slipped out?" another man said.

"Naw! That's gotta be somebody else. Huntin', maybe."

"In this rain?"

We eased up a step, then another. In a sheltered place in the lee of a rock stood two of the Fetchen outfit. I knew neither one of them by name, but I had seen them both before. In front of them was a grassy slope that fell gradually away for about fifty feet, then dropped off sharply.

The two stood there, their rifles leaning against the rock wall, well to one side, and out of the wet. They were sheltered by the overhang, but could watch a good distance up and down the canyon. One man was rolling a cigarette, the other had a half-eaten sandwich in his hand.

Taking a long step forward, rifle leveled, I turned squarely around to face them. Galloway stepped up beside me, but several feet to my right. One of them noticed some shadow of movement or heard some sound and started to turn his head.

"Just you all hold it right where you stand," I said. "We got itchy fingers, and we don't mind burying a couple of you if need be."

Neither of them was in shape to reach for a gun fast, and they stood there looking mighty foolish. "Go up to 'em, Galloway," I said, "and take their hardware. No use tempting these boys into error."

Galloway went around behind them, careful to keep from getting between my rifle and them. He slipped their guns from the holsters, and gathered their rifles. Then we backed them into the full shelter of the slight overhang and tied them hand and foot.

"You boys set quiet now. If any of the Fetchens are alive when this is over, they can come and turn you loose. But if we should happen to see you again, and not tied — why, we'd just naturally have to go to shootin'."

"If I ever see you two again," one of them said, "I'll be shootin' some my own self!"

So we left them there, scouted around, found their horses, and turned them loose. Then we went on up the mountain, careful-like. It wasn't going to be that easy again, and we knew it.

Suddenly, from up the mountain there came

223

another rifle shot, and then a scream of mortal agony. And then there was silence.

"What's going on up there, Flagan?" Galloway said. "We got somebody on our side we don't know about?"

He pointed up the hill. Three men were working their way down the hill toward us, but their attention was concentrated on whatever lay behind them. Once one of them lifted his rifle to fire, then lowered it, as if his target had vanished.

Again he lifted his rifle, and as he did so I put my rifle butt to my shoulder. If we had a helper up yonder he was going to find out it worked both ways.

"Hold your fire!" one of them called.

It was Colby Rafin, and with him was Norton Vance and two other men. They had us covered, and were close upon us.

This was no time to be taken prisoner, so I just triggered my shot and spun around on them. Galloway knew I wasn't going to be taken, and he hadn't waited. He had his rifle at his hip and he fired from there. It was point-blank range and right into the belly of Norton Vance.

He snapped back as if he'd been rammed with a fence post, then sat down and rolled over, both hands clutching his midsection.

A bullet whipped by my ear, burning it a little, but I was firing as fast as I could lever the shots. I missed a couple even at that range, for I was firing fast into the lot of them with no aim, and I was moving so as to give them no target, but I scored, too.

I'd shot at Rafin and missed him, the bullet taking the man who stood behind and to his right, and Rafin dived into the brush with lead spattering all around him. As soon as Colby Rafin got turned around he'd have us dead to rights, so we scrambled out of there and into the brush.

We moved in further, then lay still, listening.

For a time we heard no sound. Then behind us we heard a groan, and somebody called for Rafin, but he wasn't getting any answer.

We moved on, angling up the hill toward the edge of the pass. Then a burst of firing sounded below us where we'd left the rest of our party, and we stopped to look back down the hill. We could see nothing from where we were, but the firing continued. It made a body want to turn and go back, but what we had to do was what we'd started to do − clean up the pass.

They hit us just as we started to go on. During those distracting moments, few as they were, they had somehow moved down on us, and they weren't asking questions.

They just opened fire.

A bullet caught me on the leg and it buckled, probably saving my life, for there was a whipping of bullets all around me, and another one turned me sideways. I felt myself falling and tucked my shoulder under so I could roll with it, and I went over twice on the slope before I stopped.

What had happened to Galloway, I didn't know. I did know that I'd been hit hard, and more than once, and unless I moved from where I was I'd be dead within minutes. Somehow I'd clung to my rifle — I'd needed to hang onto something. Now I began to inch my way along the steepening face before me.

Instinctively, for I surely can't claim to much thinking just then, hurting the way I was, I worked back toward those hunting me. They would be off to my right, I was sure, and would think I'd try to get away, which was the smart and sensible thing. But I wanted to stay within shooting distance at any cost, and my best chances of getting away free would be to work right close to them.

But then I almost passed out. For a moment there consciousness faded, and when I snapped out of it I knew I couldn't risk that again. I had to find a place to hole up.

Crawling on, I'd gone no more than a dozen

feet before I saw what I wanted, maybe sixty feet further along. It was at a steep place on the mountainside where a boulder had jarred loose and tumbled off down the slope into the pass below, leaving a great empty socket overgrown by brush that had once hung over the boulder. If I could only get into that hollow . . .

Hours later I awakened, shaking with chill. I was curled up in that hollow and I still had my rifle. I had no memory of getting there, no idea how long it had taken me. It was nighttime now, and I was cold and hungry, and hurt.

There was room to sit up. Easing myself around, I touched my leg gingerly, feeling for the wound. One bullet had gone through my leg about five or six inches above the knee and had come out on the other side.

In here I had a hole about six feet either way, and though it was raining outside it was snug and dry here. The branches in front hung almost to the ground and, breaking off some of those on the underside, I wove them into a tighter screen. There was some bark and dry wood around the base of the tree back of the hole, but I didn't want to chance a fire.

Try as I might, there was just no way I could get comfortable. Hour after hour I lay there, huddled in the cold and the damp, trying to see my way out of this trouble. Come daylight, those Fetchen boys would be hunting my hide, and unless the rain washed out the mess of tracks I must have laid down by crawling and losing blood, they'd have me for sure.

The night and the rain are often friendly things to fugitives, but it gave me small comfort to sit there with my teeth rattling like ghost bones in a hardwood cupboard, and a gnawing pain in my thigh and another in my side.

After a time I dug out a mite more of dirt with my hands, made a hollow for my hipbone, and snuggled down on my unwounded side. I must have slept then, and when I woke up it was still dark but there was no rain — only a few drops falling from leaves. I felt that I was living on short time.

But the thing that worried me most was Galloway. Had they killed him right off? That I couldn't believe. But where could he have gotten to?

Right then I'd taken out my six-shooter and checked every load. I did the same with my Winchester, and added a few rounds to bring her up to capacity. If the Fetchen boys found me they were going to lose scalps rooting me out of here.

Then I sat back to wait. I would have liked a cup of coffee . . . four or five cups, for I'm a coffee-drinking man. But all I could do was wait and think.

That Judith girl, now. She was a mighty pretty thing, come to think of it. How could I have been so dumb as not to see it . . . Mighty contrary and ornery, though. And those freckles . . . She was pert, too pert. . . .

Other thoughts were in my mind, too. How long could those boys hold out down below — Moss, Cap, and the others?

I had to hand it to Black Fetchen. He was a general. We seemed to be winning a round or two, but all the while he was baiting trap for us.

I wished I knew what had happened to Galloway. He might be dead, or he might be lying up somewhere, worse off than me. Far down the slope I heard a long "halloo" — no voice I knew. All right, let them come.

I twitched around and studied my layout by the coming daylight. They couldn't get at me from behind, and nobody was coming up that slope in front of me. What they had to do was come right along the same way I had. Taking sight down the trail, I figured I had it covered for fifty yards; then there was a bend which allowed them cover. I had the side of the canyon for a hundred yards further along.

It started to rain again, a cold drizzle that drew a sheet of steel mesh across the morning.

The grass and the trees were greener than I had ever seen them, the trunks of the trees like columns of iron. For a long time I saw no movement. When I did see it down the trail I saw it half asleep, but I was startled into wakefulness by it.

On a second look I saw nothing, yet something had moved down there, something black and sudden, vanishing behind a bend in the trail even as it registered on my consciousness.

I lifted my rifle muzzle, and rested it on my half-bent knee. My hand was on the action as I watched the trail. My ears were alert to catch any sound, and I waited for what would come. . . .

Supposing I could get out of this jam — and all the time I knew how slight my chances were — what could I do with my future? Well, Tyrel had no more when he came west, and now he was a well-off man, a respected man, with a fine wife and a ranch.

My eyes had not wandered from the trail, and now a man came into view down there. He was following some sort of trail, although mine must have washed out long since, and he was edging closer. From his manner, it seemed to me that he fancied he was close upon whatever he was hunting.

Once, while my rifle held him covered, he

paused and started to lift his own weapon. He was looking at something above and back of me, but evidently he was not satisfied with his sight picture or else he had been mistaken in his target, for he lowered the rifle.

He came on another step, seemed then to stagger, and he started to fall even as the sound of a shot went booming down the canyon, losing itself in the rain.

The man went down to the ground, his rifle still gripped in his hand, and he lay there sprawled out not sixty yards away from me. I could see the bright stain of blood on his skull and on the trail beside him.

Who had fired?

Waiting for a minute, I saw no one, but suddenly I knew I could not stay where I was. I had taken time to plug and bind my wounds as best I could, but I desperately needed help. So, using my rifle for a crutch, I crawled from my shelter and hobbled into the cold rain.

For a few moments I would be invisible to whoever was up there. With care I worked around and started to go on up the narrow trail. I could not see anybody, but visibility was bad; I knew that shot could not have come from far off.

The trail became steeper. Hobbling along, I almost fell, then I pulled up under some trees.

"Flagan?" came the voice.

It was Judith.

She was standing half behind the black trunk of a spruce, partly shielded by its limbs. She wore a man's hat and a poncho. Her cheeks glistened in the rain and her eyes seemed unnaturally large. She must have been out on the mountain all night long, but I never saw anybody look so good.

"Be careful," she warned. "They are all around us."

"Have you seen Galloway?" I asked.

"No."

I moved up toward her, but stopped to lean against a tree. "I've been hit, a couple of times," I said. "How is it above us?"

"They are all along the ridge. I don't know how I managed to slip through," she said.

Looking up toward the ridge through the branches, I could see nothing but the trees, the rain, and the low rain clouds.

"I've got a place," she said. "We'd better get to it."

She led the way, and before she'd taken half a dozen steps I could see she knew what she was about, holding to cover and low ground, taking no chance of being seen. It was obvious she had used the route before, and that worried me. With a canny enemy against you, it never pays to go over the same ground twice. Somebody is likely to be waiting for you.

"How do you happen to be over here?" I asked her.

"Nobody came back, and we were worried. Finally I couldn't stand it any longer, so I slipped away and came in this direction."

The place she had found wasn't much more than a shelter from the rain. A lightning-struck tree had fallen almost to the ground before being caught between two others. Wedged there, it formed a shelter that she had improved by breaking off small branches on the underside and weaving them into the top.

The steep bank behind and the trees kept it dry, and she could enter it without being seen. The trees lower down the slope screened it in front, and we felt we could even have a small fire without it being seen or the smoke attracting attention.

"Flagan?" She was on the ground beside the fire, waiting for coffee water to boil.

"Yes?"

"Let's just ride away from here. I don't want to fight any more. I don't want trouble."

"You pa's down there." I gestured toward the base of the mountain, almost within view from here. "He's almighty tired, but when I left them they were holed up in a good spot."

"I want to see him, but I'm scared for you. Black will never rest until he's killed you, Flagan. You and Galloway."

"We don't kill easy."

When the coffee was ready, we drank some, and nothing ever tasted so good. But I was worried. The Fetchens were close around somewhere on this mountain, and I knew I wasn't going to get another chance. The next time we met, it had to be all or nothing. Hurt as I was, I knew I couldn't last very long.

Putting down my coffee cup, I checked my guns. Just then somewhere up the slope a branch cracked, and we both heard it.

Taking up my cup again in my left hand and keeping my six-gun in my right hand, I looked over at her. "You get down behind that mess of branches. This here is going to be a showdown."

"You scared, Flagan?"

"I guess I am. I'm not as sharp as I should be, this here wound and all." I finished my coffee. "That tasted good."

With my rifle I pushed myself up, holstered my gun, and wiped off the action of my rifle, flicking the water away. Standing on a small mound of dirt pushed up by the roots of the fallen tree, I looked down the slope.

They were coming all right. I counted five of them. And there were others up the slope, too, closing in. There must have been fourteen or fifteen in all.

"This here's going to be quite a fight," I said. "You got a pistol besides that rifle?"

She tossed it to me and I caught it left-handed and put it back of my belt.

"What are you going to do?"

"Wait until they get closer. They want a showdown, they'll have it. When they get up close I'm going to step out and go to shooting."

There wasn't anything else to do. I wasn't able to go any further, and I wasn't of a mind to. Right here we would settle it, Black and me and the rest of them.

Right here, on this wet ground we were going to fight . . . and some of us would die.

Chapter 16

At a time like that you don't count the odds, and I had the odds against me, no matter what. It wasn't as if I had a choice. This was one time when there was no place to run. It was root hog or die, and maybe both.

But seeing them coming at me, I didn't feel like dying, and I wasn't even feeling that the odds were too great. I'd come to a place and a time where it no longer mattered, and I was only thinking about how many I could take, just how I ought to move, and which targets I should choose first.

My eyes searched for Black. He was the one I most wanted to get into my sights. And in the back of my mind I was thinking: Where was Galloway?

Judith waited there behind me, and I could feel her eyes upon me. "Flagan?' she said.

"Yes?"

"Flagan, I love you."

Turning my head, I looked at her. "I love you, too," I said. "Only we haven't much time. . . . When this fuss begins, Judith, you stay out of it, d' you hear? I can make my fight better if I know you're out of harm's way."

"All right." She said it meekly enough, and I believed her.

They came on, carrying their rifles up, ready to throw down on anything that moved.

It gave me time to pick my targets — to figure my first shot, and to see just how much I'd have to move my rifle for a second. The way I figured, I had two shots before they could get me in their sights, and if I fired those two and then threw myself down I could move along the ground and get at least one more before they located me. What followed would depend on how they came up shooting, and whether they took shelter or came on.

There was no way of telling whether they had located us yet or not, only they knew we were somewhere along that slope. At first I'd been ready to step out and go to shooting as soon as they got within easy range, but then I began to figure if there wasn't some way to make the situation work for me. So much of any fight depends on the terrain and how a body uses it.

They were coming up from below and coming down from above, and we had the canyon behind us and no way out that we could see. But there was a dip of low ground running diagonally down the mountainside. It was shallow, and partly cloaked with brush, but it was deep enough so a crouching man might slip along it unseen.

If I did step out and go to shooting, I could start downhill, fire my shots, then drop into that hollow and go back up the mountain on an angle, under cover. From where they were, I doubted if they could see that low place, which had likely been scooped out by a rock slide with a lot of snow and weight behind it. With luck, I might make the hollow, get under cover, and come out where they least expected me.

All the time my thoughts kept shifting to Galloway. Common sense told me he must be dead, but there was something in me that refused to accept it. I knew Galloway, who was a tough man to kill.

The men below were well out in the open now, and they were coming along slow. Looking up, I could see the line of the ones above, spaced at intervals and coming down slope, but they could not see each other yet.

"I want to come with you," Judith said.

With my rifle, I pointed the way. "See that long gouge? If there's a way out, it will be up that way. When I shoot, or anybody else does, you hit the ground and scramble. Just keep going up that low place — there's brush all around it and they may not realize it's there. I'll be right behind you."

The time was now.

Rifle up and ready, I stepped out. Judith scooted by me and was into that shallow place before they could glimpse her. I took another quick step, brought up my rifle just as they saw me, and caught a man in my sights who wore a gray Confederate coat. The rifle jumped in my hands, the report came smashing back, and I was already shifting aim. My timing was right, and my second shot was following the first before the report died away; and then, with lead flying all around me, I took a running dive into the brush.

Branches tore at my face. I hit rolling, came up in a crouch, and made three fast steps before I caught a glimpse of an opening and a Fetchen with his rifle on me. There was no time for aiming, so I simply turned my body slightly and fired from the hip. A rifle bullet hit the tree near me and splattered my face with bark, but my bullet scored a hit ... not a killing hit, but it turned the man around in his tracks, and I was off and running, going uphill with great leaps. Twice I fell, once I lost hold my rifle, grabbed it again, and ran on. My breath tore at my lungs . . . it was the going uphill and the altitude. I slipped and fell again, felt the hammer of bullets in the earth ahead of me, rolled over under a bush, and wormed out on the other side.

That time I made three steps, but they were closing in on me. Half raised, I fired blind, left and right, and drew a smashing hail of bullets; I was just hoping they would kill each other.

Somebody hollered, and the shooting eased off. I heard them calling back and forth. They had me located, but I kept on squirming along the hollow. It seemed almost like a deer or varmint trail.

A rifle blasted somewhere up ahead, somebody cried out, and I slid across a wet boulder, hit a stretch of sand in the watercourse beyond, and managed four plunging steps before I fell, mouth open − my lungs seemed to be tearing apart.

Fear had wiped out the pain from my wounded leg, but I realized it was bleeding again. My pants leg was soaked and I could feel the squishing in my shoe, although a part of it was rain water.

There was a lot of shooting now. Judith must have opened fire from some place above me. Bleeding or not, exhausted or not, I knew it was death to stay where I was, so I scrambled. I could hear them all around me.

As I squirmed between two boulders, one of the Fetchen men reared up right before me and I hit him with my rifle butt. It wasn't much of a blow, because I held the rifle one-handed and I just swung it up from where it was.

He grabbed the rifle with both hands. But instead of trying to pull it away, I held it hard against him and swung my foot and kicked him under the chin. He went over backwards and I jerked the rifle away. He looked up at me for one black, awful instant, but it was kill or be killed, and I gave him the rifle butt in the face with both hands.

Holding up there, gasping for breath, I fed a few cartridges into the magazine of my rifle. My belt was running shy, so I reached down and ripped the belt off the Fetchen man.

Rain was pouring down, and the firing had let up. Nobody seemed to be moving, and I worked my way slowly ahead, nearing the crest of the ridge. Here and there the bottom of the gouge was choked with brush, and there were many rocks, polished by running water and the abrasion of other tumbling stones.

Once, crawling through the brush, I suddenly felt myself growing weaker, and almost blacked out. I fought against the dizziness for a moment, and then somehow I came out of it, and crawled on.

They had come in behind me now, closing off the way back, even if I had been willing or able to take it. I could hear them coming on, taking their time, checking every clump of brush or rocks.

There was no longer any question of running. I could pull myself up, and by using the rocks and brush I could remain erect long enough to move forward a few feet.

Then the ridge was close above me. I could see the bare wet rocks, the stunted cedars, and the occasional bare trunks of pines shattered by lightning.

At that moment I looked around. Four men were standing not much more than fifty feet away, aiming their rifles at me. Desperately, I threw myself to one side and fired my rifle at them. Fired, worked the lever, and fired again.

Bullets smashed into the ground around me. My hat was swept from my head, blood cascaded into my eyes, and my rifle was struck from my hand. I grabbed for it, and through the haze of blood from a scalp wound I saw that the action was shattered and useless.

Throwing the rifle down, I grabbed my six-shooter. Somehow, in throwing myself to one side, I had gotten into the cover of a rock.

A man came running down the gully, but the earth gave way and he slid faster than he expected, stones and rubble crashing down before him. I shot at point-blank range, my bullet striking the V of his open shirt and ranging upward through him.

He fell forward. I grabbed at his rifle, but it slipped away and fell down among the rocks.

Up ahead of me there was a shattering burst of gunfire — it sounded like several guns going. They must have caught up with Judith.

I could hear the ones close by talking as I waited. They were hunting me out, but they could not see me, a fact due more to the rocks where I lay than to any skill on my part. After the sudden death of the man who had slid down among the rocks they were wary, hesitant to take the risk . . . and I was just as pleased.

Right about then I must have passed out for a minute. When I opened my eyes again I was shaking with cold. The wind had come up, and was blowing rain in on me. I didn't have what you'd call shelter, just the slight overhang of a slab of fallen rock.

My hands felt for my guns. I had both pistols, and I reloaded the one right there. All the time I was listening, fighting to keep my teeth from chattering, and the knowledge growing in me that it would be almighty cold up here at night.

Nothing moved; only the rain whispered along the ground and rattled cold against the rocks. Even if I couldn't get out of this, I had to find a safer place.

On the downhill side there was a scattered stand of pine, stunted and scraggly, along with the boulders and the low-growing brush. On the uphill side there was even less cover, but the gouge up which I'd been crawling ran on for sixty yards or so further, ending just off the ridge.

It stood to reason that if they wanted me they could get me crossing that ridge. All they had to do was hold their fire and let me get out on the bare rock.

But Judith, unless she was dead or captured, was up there somewhere.

So I crawled out of shelter, over a wet boulder and along the downhill side of a great old deadfall, the log all turned gray from the weather. Maybe I made fifteen feet before I stopped to catch my breath and breathe away the pain; then I went on.

I was nearing the end of the gouge. The only thing for me to do now was break out and run for it. And I couldn't run.

Only I had to. I had to make it over that ridge. Lying there shivering in the cold rain, I studied that ridge and the ground between. Thirty steps, if I was lucky.

There was no sense in waiting. I came off the ground with a lunge, stabbing at the ground with my good leg, but hitting easy with the wounded one. I felt a shocking pain, and then I was moving. I went over the ridge and dropped beside a rock, and there they were, the lot of them.

There was Judith too, her hands held behind her, and a man's dirty hand clasped tight over her mouth so she couldn't call out to warn me. There were six of the Fetchen gang, with Black right there among them – Black and Colby Rafin.

At times like that a man doesn't think. There's no room for thought. I was soaked to the hide, bedraggled as a wet cat, bloody and sore and hurt and mad, and when I saw that crowd I did the last thing they expected.

I went for my gun.

Oh, they had guns on me, all right! But they were too busy feeling satisfied with themselves at setting the trap, and there's such a thing as reaction time. A man's got to realize what is happening, what has to be done, and he has to do it, all in the same moment.

My right hand slapped leather and came up blasting fire. And almost at the same instant my left hand snaked the other Colt from my waist-band.

There was no time for anything like choosing targets. I shot into the man right in front of me, shifted aim, and blasted again. I saw Judith twisting to get free, and pulling Rafin off balance.

Somebody else was shooting, and I saw Galloway, leaning on a crutch and his gun leaping with every spout of flame. And then, as suddenly as it began, it was over. There was a scrambling in the brush, then silence, and I was stretched out on the rocks and the rain was pounding on my back.

It seemed like hours later that I got my eyes open and looked around.

There was a fire in a fireplace, and Judith was sitting in front of it, watching the flames. I never saw anything so pretty as the firelight on her face, and catching the lights of her hair.

I was stretched out in a bunk in some sort of a low-roofed cabin, and the floor was littered with men, all apparently sleeping. Coffee was on the fire, and by the look of the coals we'd been here quite a spell.

I felt around for my gun and found it, but the rustling drew Judith's attention. She came over to me. "Ssh! The others are all asleep."

"Was that Galloway that showed up? Is he all right?"

"He's been hurt. He was shot three times, and has a broken foot. Pa's here, and so are Cap and Moss."

"Walker?"

"He's dead. He was killed, Flagan."

"Black?"

"He got away. He was hurt, I know that. You hit him once at least. He ran, Flagan. He turned and ran."

"That ain't like him."

"He was a coward," she insisted bitterly. "For all his talk, he was a coward."

"I don't believe it," I said. And I didn't believe it either. He was a lot of things, that James Black Fetchen, but he was no coward in a fight. He hated too much for that. He might have turned and run — she said he had, and she would tell me the truth — but I was sure there was more to it than that.

The old prospector's cabin where we had found shelter was on the eastern slope, not more than half a mile from where the fight had taken place.

We stayed right there a day and a half, until Evan Hawkes and Tom Sharp brought a wagon up Medano Pass. They built stretchers, and three of us came off the mountain that way.

Two weeks later I was able to sit on the porch outside the trading post and watch folks go by. Galloway was still laid up, but he was coming along fine. Though Costello was still sick, he was looking better. Cap and Moss, like the tough old-timers they were, looked about the same.

We got the news bit by bit. Three of the Fetchens had pulled out for Tennessee. Tirey was dead ... he'd been killed up on the mountain. And they hadn't found the Reynolds treasure. Like a lot of folks who've looked for it before and since, they just couldn't locate it. They had all the landmarks and they had a map, but they found nothing.

"I've seen four maps of that Reynolds treasure," Sharp told me, "and no two of them alike."

Nobody saw any of the Fetchens around, but after a few days we heard they were camped over at the foot of Marble Mountain, with several of them laid up, and at least one of them in bad shape.

Galloway limped around, still using the crutch he had cut for himself up on the mountain. Costello filled us in on all that happened before we got there.

The Fetchens had just moved in on him and he had welcomed them as guests, although mistrusting their looks. Well, they were hunting the Reynolds treasure, all right, but they wanted his ranch and Judith as well.

Costello had had a lead on that treasure himself, but it didn't pan out, and so he had settled down to hunting wild stock and breeding them to horses brought from the East, the way Tom Sharp was doing.

"Reynolds buried some loot, all right," Costello said, "but whoever finds it will find it through pure dumb luck. I don't trust any of those maps."

"They aren't cured," Moss Reardon said. "There's supposed to be treasure in a cave up on Marble Mountain too. I'd lay a bet they're huntin' it now."

For the first time in my life I was pleased just to sit and contemplate. I'd lost a lot of blood and used myself in a hard way, and so had Galloway. As I looked around that country it made me wish I had a place of my own, and I said as much to Galloway.

"We get up and around," I said, "we ought to find us a place, some corner back in the hills with plenty of green grass and water."

James Black Fetchen seemed to me like somebody from another world. After a week had passed we never mentioned the big fight on the mountain, nor any of that crowd. One thing we did hear about them. The Fetchens had buried another man somewhere up on Grape Creek.

My appetite came back, and I began thinking about work. Galloway and me had used up the mite of cash we'd had left and had nothing but our outfits. I mentioned it to Tom Sharp.

"Don't worry about it," he said. "You just eat all you're of a mind to. Those men would have caused plenty of trouble for us if you hadn't taken their measure."

The next morning we heard about the stage holdup over on the Alamosa trail.

Four men, all masked, had stopped the stage and robbed the passengers. There was no gold riding the boot on that trip, and the passengers were a hard-up lot. The robbery netted the outlaws just sixty-five dollars.

Two days later there was another holdup in the mountains west of Trinidad. That netted the thieves about four hundred dollars. There had been six of them in that lot, and one of the passengers had ridden the other stage and said they were the same outfit. One of them had been riding a big blaze-faced sorrel that sounded like Russ Menard's horse.

Sitting around waiting to get my strength back, I hadn't been idle. I'd never been one to waste time doing nothing, so while I sat there I plaited a rawhide bridle for Sharp, mended a saddle, and fixed some other things.

Costello rode out to his ranch. His place had been burned, even his stacked hay, and all the stock in sight had been driven off.

Galloway had taken to wearing two guns, one of them shoved down behind his waistband.

Then there was a holdup near Castle Rock, to the north; and word came down that Black Fetchen had killed a man at Tin Cup, a booming mining camp.

Meanwhile, Galloway and me were beginning to feel spry again, and we helped Tom Sharp round up a few head of cattle and drive them down to Walsenburg. There we heard talk of the Fetchen outlaws.

Those days Galloway and me were never far apart. We knew it was coming. The trouble was, we didn't exactly know what to expect, or when.

Costello hired two new hands, both on the recommendation of Rodriguez and Sharp. One was a Mexican named Valdez, a very tough man and a good shot who, as a boy, had worked for Kit Carson; and the other was Frank White, a one-time deputy sheriff from Kansas. Both were good hands and reliable men.

Judith was riding with me one day when she said, "Flagan, you and Galloway be careful now. I'm scared."

"Don't worry your pretty head. We'll ride loose and careful."

"Do you think he'll come back?"

Now, I was never one to lie or to make light of trouble with womenfolks. There's men who feel they should, but I've found women stand well in trouble, and there's no use trying to make it seem less than it is. They won't believe you, anyway.

"He'll come," I said. "He wasn't scared, Judith. He just wanted to be sure he lived long enough to kill Galloway and me. I've got an idea he's just waiting his chance."

By now Galloway and me were batching it in a cabin on Pass Creek. We had built up the corral, made some repairs in the roof, and laid in a few supplies bought on credit at the trading post. Work was scarce, but we disliked to leave the country with Black Fetchen still around . . . and of course, there was Judith.

We had talked about things, even made some plans, but I had no money and no immediate way of getting any. Evan Hawkes had sold out and gone back to Texas. The loss of the boy had hurt him more than he had ever showed. We were just waiting, shooting our meat out in the hills and occasionally prospecting a little.

The showdown came all of a sudden, and by an unexpected turn.

A short, stocky man came riding up to the place one day, and he had a big, black-haired man with him. Both of them were dressed like city folks, except they wore lace-up boots.

"Are you the Sacketts? Flagan and Galloway?" the short man asked.

Now, I didn't take to these men much, but they were all business. "Understand you've had trouble with the Fetchen outlaws? Well, I've got to ride the stage to Durango, and I'll need some bodyguards."

"Bodyguards?" I said.

"I'll be carrying twenty thousand dollars in gold, and while I can use a gun I am no gun-fighter, nor is my partner here. We'd like to hire you boys to ride with us. We'll pay you forty dollars each for the ride."

Now, forty dollars was wages for a top hand for a month, and all we had to do was sit up on the cushions in that stage and see that no harm came to Mr. Fred Vaughn and his money. His partner was made known to us as Reed Griffin.

We taken the job.

Chapter 17

Walsenburg was quiet when we rode in and stabled our horses. We had come up a day early, for we both needed a few things and we hadn't been close to a town since the fight. The trading post at Buzzard Roost had most things a body could wish for, but we both figured to buy white shirts and the like to wear to Durango.

We found a table in a back corner of the restaurant and hung our hats on the rack. The food was good, and the coffee better. We were sitting where we could look out the window and down the street, and we were sitting there when we saw Reed Griffin come out of a saloon down the street.

"Might as well let him know we're here," I said, but when I started to get up, Galloway stopped me.

"Plenty of time for that," he said.

Griffin walked across the road and went down a passage between two buildings and disappeared.

It was quiet where we were, and we continued to sit there, talking possibilities. We figured to prospect around Durango a mite and see what jobs were available, if any. If there were none, we would use what cash we had to outfit ourselves and go wild-horse hunting. There was always a good market for saddle stock that had been rough-broken, and while many of the wild horses were scrubs there were always a few good ones in every herd.

Later in the afternoon we went across the street to the hotel and hired ourselves a room on the second floor, in back. Pulling off our boots, we stretched out for a rest. When I woke up it was full dark, but there was a glow coming through the windows from the lights in the other buildings.

Without putting on my boots I walked across the room and poured cold water into the bowl and washed my face and combed my hair by the feel of it. I had picked up my boots and dropped into a chair by the window when I happened to look out.

The door of a house on the street back of the hotel was standing open and there were two men seated at a table over a bottle. One of those men was Colby Rafin. The other was Reed Griffin.

"Galloway?" I said, not too loud.

He was awake on the instant. "Yeah?"

"Look."

He came over and stood beside me and we looked out of our dark window and into that open door. Reed Griffin was on his feet now, but as he turned away from Rafin he was full in the light.

"Now, what d' you know about that?" Galloway said softly. "I'd say we've got to move quiet as mice."

We ate at the restaurant that night, but we fought shy of the saloons, and in the morning, right after breakfast, we were waiting at the stage stop.

Mr. Fred Vaughn was already there. He had a carpetbag and a iron-bound box with him. The stage driver loaded the box as if it was heavy, then Vaughn got in and Griffin came out and joined him. We loitered alongside, watching folks come up to the stage. There was another man, a long-geared, loose-jointed man with a big Adam's apple and kind of sandy hair. He carried a six-shooter in a belt holster, and a Winchester.

The last man to enter was lean and dark-haired. He shot us a quick, hard look, then got in. His boots were worn and his pants looked like homespun. We had never seen him before, but he had a Tennessee or maybe Missouri look about him.

The stage driver was a fat, solid-looking man with no nonsense about him, and he was obviously well known to everybody else, if not to us. We got in last and sat down facing Griffin and Vaughn, with the Tennessee man beside us; the sandy-haired man was across the way. The stage took off, headed west.

We both carried Winchesters and our belt guns, but each of us had a spare six-shooter tucked behind our waistbands. Griffin and Vaughn wasted no time talking, but made themselves comfortable as possible and went to sleep. The sandy man settled down too, although he kept measuring us with quick looks, and the man beside us as well.

The road was rough. The stage bounced, jolted, and slid over it, and every time we slowed the dust settled over us in a thick cloud.

Both of us were thinking the same thing. Why hadn't Vaughn taken the train? It ran west as far as Alamosa now, and much of our route by train ran parallel to it. In fact, the stage line was going out of business soon. This made no sense. . . . Unless there was something that could be done on the stage that could not be done on the train.

La Veta lay ahead. Once, not long ago, it had been the end of the railroad tracks, and a wild, wild town. Now the end-of-the-line boys had moved to Alamosa, although a couple of dives still remain there. To most people in this part of the country it was still simply the Plaza.

The hunch came to me suddenly, and my elbow touched Galloway ever so gently. I had noticed that Reed Griffin did not seem to be really asleep, though his eyes remained closed. My eyes went to Vaughn. He was also shamming sleep. The Tennessee man beside me was unfastening a button on his coat. Sandy was completely awake. He was watching me with bright, hard eyes, and his hand stayed close to his pistol butt.

When we got to the Plaza we changed horses, and I noticed that the Tennessee man disappeared into the stable there. Shortly after he returned, a man came from the stable, mounted a horse, and rode off down the road along which we would soon travel.

The stage driver stood by with a cup of coffee in his hands, watching the teams being switched. Strolling over to him, I said, "You size up like an honest man."

"I am that," he said coolly, "so don't make any mistakes."

"I won't, but some others will. Mister, if you hear a shot or a Texas yell from inside the stage, you let those horses run, d' you hear?"

He gave me a quick look. "What do you know?"

"I'm Flagan Sackett. That there's my brother. I think the Fletchen gang plan to take us, or kill us. And probably rob your stage in the process."

"Now I'm told. There's no law at the Plaza now."

"We'll handle it. You just run the legs off that team."

"All right," he said.

Indicating the sandy man, I asked, "Do you know him?"

"El Paso to Denver, Durango to Tucson. That's all I know. My guess is that he's a Ranger, or has been one."

He walked back inside with his coffee cup and the Tennessee man strolled over and got into the stage. Vaughn and Griffin followed. The sandy man threw down his cigarette and rubbed it out with his toe. I took one step over so he had to come up close to me, and when he drew abreast I said, "Stay out of it. The trouble's ours."

He turned his eyes on me. "You're a Sackett, aren't you? That's why you are familiar. I rode with McNelly at Las Cuevas. Orlando Sackett was there. He was a good man. I won money on him once when he fought in the ring."

"They've set us up," I said. "Everybody in that stage but you and us is safe enough," I said. "They'll stop us on the grade, I think, near Muleshoe."

The stage rolled out again, and the climb before us was a long one. Gradually the team moved slower and slower. Taking my hat from my head, I lowered it into my lap, and as I did so I drew out my waistband gun and eased it down beside my leg and out of sight, then I put my hat on again.

We went on, climbing steeply. The men across from me appeared to sleep again.

The switchback was behind us, and the stage leveled out, then suddenly I heard the driver hauling on the lines, and I lifted my Colt and looked at the men across from me.

"Sit tight, if you want to live," I said.

Galloway had lunged against the Tennessee man and I saw him strip his gun from him. The Tennesseean started up, but Galloway laid the barrel of the gun alongside his skull and he fell across our knees. We pulled our legs back and let him go to the floor of the stage.

Vaughn and Griffin both started to complain, but I shut them up. "Unless you want a cracked skull," I said.

From outside we heard a familiar voice. "All right, pull up there!"

To the Texan I said, "You want to hold these boys for me? I've got some shooting to do."

"A pleasure!" he said, and meant it.

Catching the top of the door I drew myself out of the open window on my side, hesitated an instant, and dropped to the road on the balls of my feet.

Rafin walked up to the door of the stage on the other side. I could see his boots. "All right, boys," he said. "Trot them out!"

Galloway shoved the door open, knocking him back, and leaped into the road. At the same moment I stepped around the back of the stage.

Russ Menard was the first man I saw. He was on his horse, and he had a gun resting easy in his hand. Galloway had hit the dirt and, dropping into a crouch by the wheel, was shooting into Rafin. I shot over him and my bullet crossed that of Menard, who had been taken by surprise.

He shot quickly, his bullet hitting the edge of the stage-door window, and mine knocked his shoulder. Stepping wide of the door, I shot at him again. I felt the whiff of a bullet and, turning slightly, I saw Black Fetchen taking dead aim at me.

The muzzle of his gun wasn't three feet from

my head and I dived at him, going under his outstretched arm. My shoulder sent him crashing into the side of the stage. I pushed my gun against him and fired three blasting shots, and felt his body jerk with every one, then whip free.

Menard had held his fire for fear of hitting Black, but now he fired, the bullet striking my gun belt such a blow that I was knocked staggering, and it exploded a cartridge in my belt that cut a groove in my boot toe. His horse had turned sharply, and for an instant his gun couldn't bear. When it could, I was ready and shot first, Galloway's bullet crossing mine.

Menard went off his horse, hit ground on the other side, and tried to get up. He had been hit hard, but his eyes were blazing with a strange white light and his grip on his gun was steady. I shot into him again and he backed up and sat down again.

Somewhere off to my right I heard the stage driver saying, "Careful now, you with the itchy finger. This shotgun will cut you in two. Just stand fast."

Menard was sitting there looking at me, one knee sort of drawn up, his gun lying across his leg. He had been hit twice in the lungs and every time he drew breath there was a frothy burst of blood from the front of his vest.

"I told him he should leave you alone," he said, "but he wouldn't listen. I told him nobody could beat a man's luck, and you had it."

"So this is all for you," I said quietly.

"Looks like it. Pull my boots off, Sackett, and bury me deep. I don't want the varmints after me."

Not being a trusting man, I still held my gun on him while I tugged his boots free.

"You take the gun," he said. "It brought me nothing but trouble."

Galloway had come up to me. "Fetchen's dying," he said. "You tore him apart."

Taking Menard's gun, I backed off from him.

James Black Fetchen was not dying; he was dead, and there were two others besides him, one of them the man I'd seen at the stable.

The stage driver rolled his tobacco in his cheeks. "If you boys are through, we might as well bury 'em and get on. I got a schedule to keep."

At the placer-mining camp of Russell the stage pulled up and we got down. We took Reed Griffin and Fred Vaughn out on the street. "We agreed to see you safe to Durango. You had us set up for killing. Now, do you figure we've earned our money, or do we take you all the way?"

263

"You going to let us go?"

"Forty dollars each," I said, and he paid it.

"Ride out with the stage," I said, "and keep going."

So we let them go, the Texan riding along to see them on their way.

"Galloway," I said, "we'd better find some horses and ride back to that cabin on Pass Creek."

"You figure we should stay there?"

"Well, there's Judith. And that's pretty country."

"Hey, did you see that niece of Rodriguez' do the fandango? Every time I looked at her my knees got slacker'n dishwater."

We had come a far piece into a strange land, a trail lit by lonely campfires and by gunfire, and the wishing we did by day and by night. Now we rode back to plant roots in the land, and with luck, to leave sons to carry on a more peaceful life, in what we hoped would be a more peaceful world.

But whatever was to come, our sons would be Sacketts, and they would do what had to be done whenever the call would come.